Women of Trachis

Sophokles

Rachel Kitzinger and Eamon Grennan,
translators

**LEVER
PRESS**

Lever Press (leverpress.org) is a publisher of pathbreaking scholarship. Supported by a consortium of liberal arts institutions focused on, and renowned for, excellence in both research and teaching, our press is grounded on three essential commitments: to be a digitally native press, to be a peer-reviewed, open access press that charges no fees to either authors or their institutions, and to be a press aligned with the ethos and mission of liberal arts colleges.

The complete manuscript of this work was subjected to a partly closed ("single blind") review process. For more information, please see our Peer Review Commitments and Guidelines at https://www.leverpress.org/peerreview

DOI: https://doi.org/10.3998/mpub.12159971
Print ISBN: 978-1-64315-030-7
Open access ISBN: 978-1-64315-031-4

Published in the United States of America by Lever Press, in partnership with Amherst College Press and Michigan Publishing

Contents

Member Institution Acknowledgments

Lever Press is a joint venture. This work was made possible by the generous support of Lever Press member libraries from the following institutions:

Adrian College
Agnes Scott College
Allegheny College
Amherst College
Bard College
Berea College
Bowdoin College
Carleton College
Claremont Graduate
    University
Claremont McKenna College
Clark Atlanta University
Coe College
College of Saint Benedict /
    Saint John's University
The College of Wooster

Denison University
DePauw University
Earlham College
Furman University
Grinnell College
Hamilton College
Harvey Mudd College
Haverford College
Hollins University
Keck Graduate Institute
Kenyon College
Knox College
Lafayette College Library
Lake Forest College
Macalester College
Middlebury College

Morehouse College
Oberlin College
Pitzer College
Pomona College
Rollins College
Santa Clara University
Scripps College
Sewanee:
    The University of the South
Skidmore College
Smith College
Spelman College
St. Lawrence University

St. Olaf College
Susquehanna University
Swarthmore College
Trinity University
Union College
University of Puget Sound
Ursinus College
Vassar College
Washington and Lee
    University
Whitman College
Willamette University
Williams College

A NOTE ON THE TRANSLATION

Translation is a tricky business. The philosopher Roman Jakobson said that *poetry is by definition untranslatable*. And the Italian phrase *tradurre tradire* (to translate [is] to betray) explains itself. Every translation, that is, has to be a "betrayal" of the original. That said, however, any translator will try to make his or her work as little a betrayal as possible. It is a starting place.

Most of us know, of course, that it was Robert Frost who said (in an oft-repeated formulation) "poetry is what gets lost in translation." No questioning the at least partial truth of that. But the translator seeks to lose not everything but to allow the new poem or play or other literary work to carry at least some of the marks that distinguish, individualize, and identify the new text as as close a family relation of the original as possible. What one tries to achieve, in other words, is a new poetry in the receiving language, one that smacks as much as possible of the texture and the flavors of the original.

Adequate translation, too, might be seen as a kind of fluent *commuting* between languages, hoping (as we go) for one kind of *equivalence* or another. But since the translator is in every sense a stumbler-after, a sense of loss has to be part of the stoical attitude with which any translator will take up the task. And though a translation may be, as has been said, "like a stewed strawberry," yet—though lacking the freshness of the original—it can still hold on to, and manifest, something essential. In the end, as Auden remarked, one has simply to recognize, in as positive a way as one can, that "Theoretically, it is impossible. One has to try." Every translation, so, is—in every sense—a trial. We try, and whether we like it or not, we are always on trial.

Impossible as it may be, then, the task of translation has to be attempted. For it is natural for readers to desire some sense of what any poem or play or other literary work in any other language, ancient or modern, means and *feels like* in their own language. Losses notwithstanding, we must try (beyond the simplifications of "translatorese") to get at what, in our own language, might be— in as many senses as possible—*going on* in the source text.

In Rachel Kitzinger and my attempt (a collaborative work between a scholar of Greek drama who is also a director of Greek plays and an Irish poet lacking knowledge of the Greek originals), we have opted for one set of possibilities, which may be seen in negative and positive ways. First, we have decided not to be "rigidly faithful" (whatever that might mean) to the original, deciding that would lead to a "faithfully rigid" version in English (and, unavoid-ably, to "translatorese").

On the positive side, we have tried in our version of *Women of Trachis* to get at a *language manner* that adheres as closely as pos-sible in English to what's going on in the original but in a manner that is our own and modern: a version that is recognizably *idiom-atic* but not *colloquial*. For we feel that the colloquial (no matter the benefits of apparent immediacy) would be at odds not only with the literary formality but also with the essential spirit of the original. We wanted to find a mode of expression that would avoid archaism, on the one hand, and the overly contemporary, on the other: idiomatic but not contemporary/colloquial.

Here is a brief extract from Deianeira's opening speech:

When I was young
still living in my father's house—
Oineus' house, in Pleuron—
I shuddered with fear more than any girl in Aitolia
at the thought of marriage. Why?
My suitor was a river, the river Acheloos!
A shape-shifting monster!
He came to ask for me from my father:
one minute he was a sleek-shouldered bull;
the next—all twists and turns—a shimmering snake;
then a man-body with the face of an ox,
clear water gushing from his bushy beard.
At the thought of marrying him
I felt nothing but misery, and I prayed I'd die
before I'd have to lie in his bed. (ll. 9–23)

What we hope you'd see, and even more *hear*, in this short passage from the beginning of the play is how the speech contains in its manner something of Deianeira's character—thoughtful, observant, plain, and immediate in her language, not overly "rhetorical" yet capable of some speed, emotional edge, and thrust (in the abrupt questions and exclamations) while remaining clear-eyed and in control (*at the thought of marrying him / I felt nothing but misery*). At the same time, it manages without strain to be *rhythmic*, true to its own sense of the modern free verse line. All of this we hope to be, in soliloquy, the introduction to a plausibly dramatic (and theatrically persuasive) character.

This remained our ambition, too, while translating the various choral odes, songs, and chants. What we sought in each of these was an emphasis on rhythm and speed of utterance (achieved by various means) that would distinguish these elements by raising the emotional temperature of what is sung or chanted

Here, from the first chorus, is a passage that will illustrate what we hope for these more deliberately calculated passages. What we sought was a more rhythmically heightened language, to convey—by rhythmic means, by absence of punctuation, by a use of language distinct from the plainer utterances of the dialogue or monologue of the characters—the more deliberately ritualistic element of the play.

> *Just as a man might see*
> *wave after wave*
> *roused by a big wind north or south*
> *rise and fall,*
> *fall and rise*
> *on the wide ocean:*
> *so a sea of trouble*
> *like that rough sea ever circling Krete*
> *casts down then raises up Theban Herakles.*
> *But some god or other*
> *always hauls the unwavering man*
> *back from the dark house of Death.* (ll. 158–69)

What we hope for such passages is that their rhythmic and syntactical formality

> *rise and fall,*
> *fall and rise*
> *on the wide ocean:*
> *so a sea of trouble*

will speak ritually to the ears of an audience or a reader, persuading them of a different *mode* of expression and suggestive of the way the chorus partakes in and yet is in important ways separate from the world in which the characters live and suffer.

In sum, what Rachel Kitzinger and I sought was to ground our translation in modern English, savoring of modern English speech. What we wanted most of all in the dialogues and monologues, as well as in the choric songs, chants, and heroic utterances, was something *speakable* (or *singable*), something dramatically (and theatrically) immediate, recognizable, and in some way close-to-home yet also in its own way strange, of its own world: a world that remains far-off but not out of sight or earshot. The *flavor*, that is, of another world, other worlds, whether the speaker speaks in plain dialogue or is delivering a chanting speech like so many of those of Herakles. Here is a fragment of a speech by the Nurse:

> *There she fell wailing before the altars*
> *crying out they'd all be deserted now.*
> *And she wept, poor woman, as one by one*
> *she touched those simple things*
> *she'd always used around the house. Now here, now there*
>
> *she wandered through the rooms*
> *and if she saw anyone—any maid or servant*
> *dear to her—she'd burst into tears at the sight of them.* (ll. 1264–72)

Straightforward in its pathos, there is no attempt, rhythmic or otherwise, to decorate or elaborate: it's a plain statement of the unhappy facts.

Here, in contrast, is a chanting passage from Herakles:

> *Who are you, you Greeks! Most unjust!*
> *For you I destroyed myself*
> *cleansing your seas, clearing your forests*
> *of all that was bad in them.*
> *And now*
> *will no one bring fire or lift a sword*
> *to relieve my pain?* (ll. 1392–98)

What we seek here is speech that is burdened with feeling: our attempt is to convey that through repetitions and declamatory exclamations, thus offering a portrait of a character in pain. In other words, we seek power and bigness of expression (Herakles is, after all, one way or another "larger than life"), but what we want to avoid is *melodrama*: we want his humanity, yes, but carried to another level.

***

To illustrate further these few points, I'll take a few examples from other translations and line them up with our own, not to decide what's better or best but simply to see, to illustrate how our own is working.

Here, so, are three small examples of the same short passage in past translations. The exchange takes place between Hyllos and Deianeira, as she encourages him to find his missing father.

First, the earliest, mostly iambic, with rhyme:

H.

But now, having the knowledge, I will do
    All things to find which of those ends be true.

D.

Go then my son. To have done the right, though late
The knowledge came, must needs be fortunate.
            Gilbert Murray, *The Wife of Heracles* (1947)

Next, a fragment from Ezra Pound's version—speedy, direct, colloquial:

H.

But now I'll go get the facts.

D.

Well, get going. A bit late, but a good job's worth a bonus.
                    Ezra Pound, *Women of Trachis* (1957)

Next, a fragment from a 1978 version: modern/contemporary but
calmer than Pound's—with the shadow of iambic at play.

H.

All right. I do know now.
I'll find the truth, no matter what.

D.

Go ahead, then. If news is good,
it does good, late or not.
                    C. K. Williams and Gregory W. Dickerson,
                    Women of Trachis (1978)

And here's a very recent version by Keyne Cheshire called *Murder
at Jagged Rock* (2015)—very colloquial, with a Wild (American) West
setting, including its slangy vocal trappings, though a bit unevenly
employed:

H.

But now I see. And Ma, I'm gonna stop at nothin'
I'll be rootin' out the truth about it all.

D.

Well go then Son. Some news avails even him
who learns it late—news what's good, at any rate.

As far as our own version is concerned, we try to position it between extremes of formality and the colloquial, and in the general area of the Williams/Dickerson version, but not as much inflected by an iambic rhythm.

H.

I'll go, Mother. Of course I will.
I'd have been with him long ago
if I'd known of these prophesies. (ll. 121–23)

D.

Go then, my son.
Even if you learn good news late,
it can still be to your advantage. (ll. 129–31)

As can be seen/heard in our version, we mostly strive in straight dialogue for more or less "normative" idiomatic speech.

***

At the same time, we want our version's language to be capable of rising beyond that ground into the more deliberately calculated zone of the lyrical, the more decisively rhythmical zones of chorus, chant, and song.

Here's a taste from the Gilbert Murray version of that aspect of the original:

Chorus.

[Music and triumphal dance.]

Leader.

O House, uplift thy voice!
And jubilate thou Hearth!
A bridal song shall cry Rejoice,
And shouts of men go forth,

Men.

To thee, of the Quiver unfailing, Apollo, the Lord of our choice.

Maidens.

And with them, O Artemis, maidens in joy shall their paean combine,
Thou torch-lit Ortygian huntress, to thee and the nymphs that are thine!

All.

A paean! A paean divine!

The deliberate beats and the overt rhymes are obvious here.

✳✳

For many reasons, and one deliberate formal choice, the same chorus from the Williams/Dickerson version sounds very different:

SOAR!
   LET THIS
      HOUSE SOAR!

HEARTH
> *CRIES! HOUSE-*
>> *CRIES! ALTAR!*

The house!
> *The husband—*
>> *hungry house,*

let it
> *SOAR!*
>> *Men!*

To Apollo
> *soar!*
>> *His brilliant*

arrow! Women! The healing
> *the healing hy*
>> *mn, Apollo!*

***

And here are roughly the same lines from the Grennan/Kitzinger version, its rhythms partly determined by the length of the line and the almost complete absence of punctuation:

> *Let the house all shout*
> *cries of joy: ululations*
> *sung at the hearth*
> *of this house that soon*
> *will celebrate a marriage!*

> *And let the men too*
> *raise together*
> *their chant to Apollo*
> *the great Protector,*
> *his quiver bright-shining.*

> *All together girls*
> *girls all together*

lift a loud paian, your paian
to Artemis his sister. (ll. 282–95)

***

As far as the verse itself is concerned, we have not tried to imitate the original verse forms, which would seem artificial if grafted onto English. At the same time, we've tried to find some heightened manner that might approximate modern verse (whether free or stanzaic), a version distinctly rhythmic, occupying its own zone of poetic, lyric elevation. In all of this, both in the "plain" and the "heightened" parts of the play, there are important and immediately obvious differences between the Murray version, the Williams/Dickerson version, and our own (most notably in the choric songs).

***

Probably the most effective modern translation at the moment is Robert Bagg's. He finds in his rendering of the choruses easy and idiomatic runs of language. Here is his sun hymn sung by the chorus:

O Sun! The Night
pulsing with stars
gives birth to you
the moment she
reddens into death.
You set, O Sun,
fire to her sky
as she lays you
to rest, O Sungod—
where, tell us where,
is Herakles,
Alkmene's child.

This is effective, though it departs from the *amplification* of the Greek choric manner. The Grennan/Kitzinger translation expands the lines for different effect:

> *O you whom shimmering Night*
> *brings forth from her plundered womb*
> *and day's end lays to blazing rest—*
> *you, Sun, you I call to:*
> *where is Alkmene's son?*
> *Where is he?* (ll. 132–37)

***

Such is a very small sampling of some of the differences between the Grennan/Kitzinger translation and some other versions. And so we offer you this, our translation of Sophokles' *Women of Trachis,* hoping it will be, as the Latin poet says, both *dulce* and *utile*: helpful and enjoyable, useful and pleasing, while also being dramatically and theatrically accessible in performance. And hoping, of course, that something of the magic, mystery, and power of the original may—from such a reading as ours—be apprehended by our student readers.

A BRIEF NOTE ON THE TRANSLATORS' COLLABORATIVE PROCESS

Only one of us has a firsthand knowledge of Greek. Rachel is a teacher and scholar of Ancient Greek. 1 am not. As in our earlier translation of Sophokles' *Oedipus at Colonus* (Oxford, 2005), the way our collaboration worked reflects and builds on what follows from this basic difference.

While 1, in preparation, read a few other translations of *Women of Trachis*, the first stages in our own translation were all Rachel's. First she moved slowly, meticulously—line by line—through the original Greek text, making notes of the literal meanings of each word, each line. After a number of drafts doing this, in order to achieve to the best of her ability an acceptable literal rendering of each word, each phrase, each line, and noting variant possibilities, she then made an interlineal primary working text, which she passed on to me.

From this working text I could see not only the literal meaning of words and phrases, but by sounding out the Greek (which I can manage roughly to do), I could get a sense of the building blocks of a passage, whether it was speech, dialogue, or choric song. Things, in other words, had been broken down for me, so I could then go bit by bit to encounter the unit in the Greek of each line, and my task was to work towards getting some sort of English equivalents for how the sense units and the line units actually work.

What I am always after at first is a way to make these sense and line units work in English. Of course, in two languages so radically different, this can only be an approximation at best, but it is always our first task. Only then can we say we are moving towards the kind of translation we are after. Often this simply means a shifting about of the syntax to achieve the English norm. So what Rachel might pass on to me at first might sound like this:

> May I not know wrong acts of daring
> may I not learn them. I despise women who have dared.
> But if in some way I might with this potion prevail over
> this girl and with these charms over Herakles
> the act has been devised—unless I seem somehow
> to act wantonly. In that case I will stop.

I would begin with this as the base, the sense foundation, as it were, and work to bring that into some sort of fluent idiomatic phrasing. This then I would pass back to Rachel.

At this point, the hard work of negotiation would begin, as we worked back and forth together to achieve a version on which both of us would agree: something that would sound natural in English (idiomatic though not deliberately colloquial) and not betray the Greek's literal meaning nor its—for want of a better word—feeling. By working on short manageable passages in this way, working them over through a number of drafts, we would then get a certain amount of the play into what we would accept as a version "to be going on with." The number of drafts we needed to achieve such satisfactorily shaped passages varied, depending on whatever cruces or disagreements we might have about what worked most adequately and what we could agree on as a true (but always, of course, "imperfect") version of the Greek text.

As a next stage along our way to completion, we recorded our version and listened to it and then did a reading of the text with some friends. This allowed us to *hear* our translation for the first time. Stemming from this, we made some adjustments—changing lines for their rhythm and sometimes changing word choice or word order. Always we were working towards a speaking text, something we believed would work for actors in dramatic, theatrical performance.

The final stage in this collaborative process was the preparation of a fully staged performance of our translation with drama students from Vassar College. Rachel worked with the student director and the cast to give them the background they needed to understand the play and then make it their own. My part was, initially, to sit in on some early rehearsals. Then, together, we worked with the five members of the chorus and the choreographer to help them find and work with the rhythms of the choral songs. Hearing these young actors speak the lines we had written was a very gratifying experience, for it gave us confidence that indeed the translation was working as we had all along hoped it would. The students didn't seem to have to struggle to make the language natural to them and invest it with their sense of the characters. The experience of hearing the play in action, then, steered us to some further revisions and, in the end, to an audio recording of the script by the student actors. Then it was on to a full-scale performance—which never happened since the COVID-19 pandemic closed the College. But, by then, having done our revisions at each stage of the way towards a complete and coherent script/text, we had achieved as well as we could what we had in collaboration set out to do.

It could be and was a concentrated, trying, time-consuming, and always demanding process, since of course we were working with different knowledge, hopes, understandings, and acoustic tunings. But we stuck to it as a means of proceeding towards what we knew our common aim was: an English version of Sophokles' text that could be spoken, would allow for dramatic and theatrical and even poetical conviction by speakers on stage and auditors in an audience.

By doing in collaboration what I have described here, we managed in the end to get to an agreed-upon, adequate translation of the whole play: a translation that Rachel could feel was—remote as it couldn't avoid being—as close to her understanding of the play as possible. And a translation that also would fairly represent what we had been after: a performable, speaking text, whether in monologue, dialogue, song, or chant. We proceeded, thus, from the first reading by Rachel, through the interlineal literal version, to the collaborative back and forth of our struggle to be true to what we both hoped the English version would achieve. What followed, then, were some hearings of the text in real voices, then through an acting version in rehearsals, then on to an actual audio recording: each stage being marked by further adjustments, big and small.

And so, after a few years of work (during which, of course, we had other tasks, duties, projects, and responsibilities to attend to), we came to what seemed to both of us a productively, and we hope persuasively, creative outcome: an adequate text/script of *Women of Trachis*, in which the initial translation I've used to begin this note appears as follows:

May I never learn—nor even consider—
wrong, reckless acts: I hate women who do.
But if somehow with this potion,
these spells over Herakles,
I might prevail over this girl,
then I've made it ready—
but if it seems I act too rashly.
I'll stop right now. (ll. 830–37)

INTRODUCTION

Why another translation of *Women of Trachis*? Of course, there is always a need for new translations; no translation can be definitive, and each new one opens up a different aspect of the work being translated, as it is mediated by a different sensibility and different choices, different emphases, offered in new rhythms, idioms, images. But this play has not been given as much attention as other Sophoklean plays; it is rarely performed and certainly appears less often on syllabuses than, say, *Oedipus Tyrannos* or *Antigone*. So we hope with this translation to spur further interest in the play among those who are interested in Greek literature and those who are interested in creating productions of Greek plays. And with this introduction, we hope to show the reader the approach to the play that has guided our translation, since all translators are, of necessity, also interpreters.

1. FOCUS AND STRUCTURE

This is not an easy play—none of the characters effortlessly engages our sympathies or respect, its plot is grim, and its structure puzzling. Compared with characters in Sophokles' other surviving tragedies, the characters in this play seem less able to assert their commitments—whether moral, political, or religious—in the context of a set of hostile circumstances. There is little sense of the human qualities that emerge, however disastrously, as meaningful responses to the fragility of the human condition in other Sophoklean plays. And yet the play dramatizes, uniquely in extant Greek tragedy, a question that addresses one of our contemporary preoccupations: How does the human condition differ for men and for women, especially in light of the various ways society constructs their roles? There are, of course, many questions the play raises, but the different circumstances and different voices and roles of the men and women characters have been in the forefront of our minds as we have translated it.

There are two structural features that invite this focus. First, each episode in the first two-thirds of the play begins with a monologue by Deianeira, the wife of Herakles. It is her point of view that focuses the audience's attention on the events being narrated. And it is her life as a woman and a wife and her relationship to Herakles that she tells us about—an unusual focus for Greek tragedy. And second, the return of Herakles to his family, an event that the play moves towards from its beginning, does not, finally, bring about the meeting of husband and wife. The "return of the hero" is a plot with powerful precedents: both Homer's *Odyssey* and Aeschylus' *Agamemnon*, which predate *Women of Trachis*, dramatize a hero's return. In both cases the meeting of man and wife is central to the plot. In *Women of Trachis*, however, despite the expectations raised by this plot type, the two never meet. Deianeira is not Penelope, keeping the house intact in preparation for Odysseus' return and eventually greeting him back into it. Nor is she Clytaemnestra, anticipating Agamemnon's return by plotting his death and killing him on his first reentering the house. In *Women of Trachis*, Deianeira and Herakles never share the same space, whether for good or ill. The male and female worlds remain deeply divided.

Sophokles thus structures his play to draw attention to and

explore the differences that keep Deianeira and Herakles apart. Before we look more closely at this difficult relationship between a wife and a husband, we should consider another thematic thread that runs through the play. Many critics have written about the way that characters come to an understanding of what has happened or is happening too late to change, or successfully deal with, the consequences of their actions. We watch the characters revise their understanding of the past or the present. Or they must reevaluate the reasons for an action they have taken, in light of information that they receive too late to prevent the painful consequences of that action. This human reality shapes the rhythm of the play, as each new revelation or reassessment of the meaning of the past propels the plot forward. Connected to this rhythm is the slow unfolding of the meaning of oracles, known but only partially understood, as if the constant revisions of understanding gradually make clear a future whose shape the oracles have revealed in little pieces, buried in shadow.

The imperfection of human knowledge and its consequences for people trying to understand and shape their lives are captured in the first lines that Deianeira speaks in the play: "You've all heard the old saying: / *There's no knowing a man's life— / has it been good? has it been bad?— / till he's dead*" (ll. 1–4). These lines express a truism, illustrated vividly, for example, by Sophokles' friend Herodotos in Book 1 of his *Histories*, when he shows Solon questioning the assumption made by Croesus, the fabulously wealthy king of Lydia, that his wealth guarantees his happiness. Not only may the gods at any moment shift the course of a life, but people themselves can take an action they think will lead to a good result, only to find that they can never know enough to be sure that action will achieve what they intend. And so the play proceeds to make this imperfection of human knowledge and understanding a constant presence, a bell sounded again and again, a rhythm of discovery and revision that is as pervasive as the air the characters breathe. Simon Goldhill has written, "Sophocles is much concerned with human's lack of control over narrative and language, and with the structure of self-deception which inform the misplaced attempt to achieve such certainty."[1] Lack of control over narrative or, using a theatrical framework, lack of control over the consequences of their actions: this is the ground, so to speak, on which all characters in Sophoklean drama walk.

But Deianeira makes herself an exception to this fact of human existence in her second sentence, when she asserts that she knows the shape of her life; she knows it is, and will be, full of misery. This claim to knowledge might strike the audience as foolish, and some critics have seen her certainty here as an example of Sophoklean irony. If it is irony, however, it is not an irony based in the character's complete misunderstanding, like the dramatic irony of the *Oedipus Tyrannos*, for example. Deianeira's pessimistic understanding about the arc of her life is confirmed by the end of the play. Both her imperfect understanding of the past and the actions she takes with inadequate knowledge in the present lead in the same direction: to confirm, to an even greater extent than she can imagine, the truth of her judgment that her life is miserable. Perhaps it *is* irony that, in fact, she cannot imagine how bad her life will be by the end of the play, but it is not an irony based in an assertion that unknowingly displays ignorance of reality.

What gives Deianeira an understanding of the shape of her life that contradicts the truism with which she opens the play and counters the theme of "learning too late"? And what does Sophokles lead the audience to consider through this contradiction? Deianeira is an exceptionally self-reflective character. Her monologues, which focus every episode until her silent, final exit two-thirds of the way through the play, offer the audience the opportunity to hear, uniquely in extant Greek tragedy, the thoughts and feelings of a wife and mother in her domestic world. Not, like Medea, for

---

1. Simon Goldhill, "Undoing in Sophoclean Drama: *Lusis* and the Analysis of Irony," *Transactions of the American Philological Association* 139.1, 2009, 47.

example, a woman expressing her feelings after her domestic world has been destroyed but a woman who narrates what it has been like to be a girl and then a woman and who then struggles before our eyes to preserve her world from the forces that threaten to destroy it. From the start, her claim to a unique knowledge about the course of her life is confirmed by the narrative she offers of a woman's condition. Her pessimistic claim is inextricably bound to her understanding of a woman's—and, in particular, a wife's—lot. In the contrast that Deianeira draws in the first few lines of the play between other people's inability to know the course of their lives and the knowledge she has of the shape of her own, the audience is challenged to wonder whether the consequences that arise from the limit in human knowledge are different for men and for women. Does Deianeira's life as it unfolds through the course of the play illuminate that difference?

2. DEIANEIRA AND THE WORLD OF WOMEN

It is a woman's voice that opens the play. There has been considerable disagreement about whom Deianeira addresses in her opening monologue. Clearly the Nurse has accompanied her out of the house. But there is no indication in Deianeira's speech that she is addressing her. (We have chosen to indicate that she addresses the Nurse only in the speech's last lines.) And, in fact, there would be little need for her to tell her nurse, who has been with her most of her life, the story she narrates. Critics have argued that it is inconceivable that a character would address the audience directly in tragedy, though it is common in comedy. But we might imagine that Sophokles is allowing his audience, in an unusually intimate way, to overhear Deianeira as she talks to herself and tries to make sense of her feelings. Like Homer in the *Odyssey*, who starts Odysseus' story with an account of Penelope in Ithaka, Sophokles starts the story of Herakles' return with the situation Herakles' long absence has created for his wife. But unlike Penelope, whose actions the narrative shows but does not interpret, Sophokles gives Deianeira a voice that focuses the audience's attention on her position in the world as a woman and allows them to see the world from her point of view. Perhaps, indeed, Sophokles opened his play in such an unusual way, with Deianeira addressing no one in particular, to make a dramatic point about the rare occurrence on the tragic stage of a woman revealing the normal conditions of her life.

Deianeira lets the audience hear, in the first two-thirds of the play, what it feels like to be a woman: how a young girl grows up in a protected space and, for the only time in her life, is free from others' eyes, others' judgments, and is secure; how it feels to be sought in marriage; what it is like to be a married woman who is in love with her husband; and, finally, what choices are available to her when her world is threatened. Her story is told in the heightened framework of a myth but can be seen as the story, writ large, of any young girl in Athens of a certain class. (We know almost nothing about the lives of "working-class" women.) She is wooed initially by an actual monster-like figure, the river Acheloos. But it is not hard to imagine that, for a young, protected girl, the man from outside her world who arrives to take possession of her could appear as monstrous as the river god does to Deianeira. Through her physical description of him, charged as it is with sexual imagery, she shows how the prospect of such a suitor feels. She narrates the rivalry between her two suitors, Acheloos and Herakles, in dramatic terms, as a battle, but the threat of violence in male rivalry must also have been an actual, lived experience for a young girl, even if the male rivals were not superhuman figures.[2]

2. In Athens at the time the play was performed, a girl, at age fourteen or fifteen, would be given (or "loaned," in the Greek terminology) by her guardian (usually her father but more generally any male figure who has legal charge of her) to a man with whose family her family wishes to make or strengthen a connection. The girl is unlikely to have had contact with men outside her family before the marriage and will not have had a chance to meet the man she is marrying before she moves from her family home to the home of her husband. The girl's unfamiliarity with the male world and with the person to whom she is being married

Some critics have interpreted her fear in the face of such rivalry as a characteristic belonging particularly to Deianeira. It seems much more likely to be a dramatized representation of most young women's normal experience. And although she says she felt relief when the less monstrous of her suitors won her, she quickly discovers a new source of fear. To be a married woman who feels not only dependence on, but also love for, her husband is to suffer constant worry for him, because he is constantly out in a world she cannot know. Again her situation is magnified by being married to Herakles, who is gone for longer periods of time and on more risky exploits than the men of the audience, citizens of Athens. But Deianeira's life is not of a different kind altogether from what many Athenian wives would experience. Whenever the play was written (and there is no agreement about when in a range of about twenty years, between roughly 450 and 430 BCE), the Athenian audience would have had either the memory of men going off to fight the Persians or the more immediate experience, as just one example, of the Athenian navy sailing frequently to the far-flung cities of the growing Athenian empire to maintain control. And indeed, even the obligation of men to engage in the more peaceful activities of *polis* life meant that they largely functioned in a world that women had no experience of and could not share. The division of men's and women's lives, between a life lived in public and a life largely kept private, respectively, and the subsequent lack of experience women had of their husbands' activities may well have led many women to worry about, or at the very least feel disconnected from, their husbands' preoccupations and well-being.[3] Such ignorance

may well have made the experience frightening. See https://www.metmuseum.org/toah/hd/wmna/hd_wmna.htm; https://oxfordre.com/classics/view/10.1093/acrefore/9780199381135.001.0001/acrefore-9780199381135-e-6892.

3. In Athens in the second half of the fifth century BCE, all free men whose parents were both Athenian were expected to participate in the running of the city-state. These duties included attending the assembly where laws were proposed and voted on, serving on juries, and being ready to fill those positions in the government that were chosen by lot, among other duties. There were also many

may also have made women's dependence on their husbands for their security a source of anxiety.

In the context of this worry, Deianeira allows the audience to experience the importance of the house as a known place, where a woman can have some control over her circumstances. Deianeira lets us see the fragility of that security and the cost of its preservation. She is living in exile—displaced from the home she has established with Herakles because of Herakles' murder of Iphitos (in Sophokles' version, anyway; other versions give other killings as the cause of the exile). So Deianeira's current situation, living in a strange place and dependent on the hospitality of others, is again an exaggerated version of the experience of any woman leaving her father's house and having to establish a home among strangers. Her ability to create and maintain her position within the house is the only form of security she has.[4]

In the course of the play, we learn that the real threat to Deianeira's sense of a secure space is Herakles' sexual desire for another

festivals and cult celebrations to attend for which attendance was expected or required. Depending on their economic status, men participated in the military either as members of the cavalry, army, or navy. Men who did not come from wealthy families would be engaged outside the house in the daily activities of farming or commerce, while men from rich families congregated in the public spaces of the city, in the gymnasia, or in the men's quarters in one another's houses to discuss, among other things, the affairs of the city and to create political alliances. Younger men were often introduced to the life and responsibilities of a citizen through an erotic relationship with an older man. See http://www.agathe.gr/democracy/athenian_citizenship.html.

4. It is important for modern readers trying to understand the desire for security that Deianeira expresses to realize that women in ancient Athens only had the possibility of living in their father's or their husband's house. For example, if a marriage ends in divorce, the wife returns to her family home. In addition, a woman had no legal standing. If she is involved in a legal dispute, she cannot represent herself but must be represented by her "guardian." Another factor that may contribute to a woman's sense of insecurity is the degree to which a woman's position can be threatened by what others say about her. While the importance of reputation is true of men as well, we can imagine that the hiddenness of women's lives makes them more subject to the vagaries of rumor and gossip.

woman, Iole. When the intensity of his desire drives him to introduce Iole into her house, Deianeira's ability to sustain the equanimity she first displayed in response to Iole's presence fails her, as she asserts would be true of any woman. Here again, the audience is taught by Deianeira to see how Iole's intrusion into the house—in essence, Herakles' first "communication" with Deianeira in over a year—shatters her sense of herself and the security of the place in which she must exist. Once again, that intrusion is extreme, surely not typical of the audience's experience. But what is typical is the imbalance in the resources available for men and for women to respond to circumstances that disrupt their lives: Herakles can take an action completely within the normal frame of his existence to ease the passion that controls him; Deianeira has to go against her better judgment and her nature to try to preserve her world from what threatens it.[5]

From Deianeira's initial reaction on meeting Iole, the audience understands how contrary to her nature it is not to be able to tolerate Iole's presence in the house. Before she knows who Iole is, Deianeira expresses deep sympathy for Iole's situation out of her understanding of their common lot as women and humans subject to the vagaries of time. Then, in a monologue following their

---

5. The only restrictions on male sexual freedom in fifth century Athens were incest and adultery. Married men engaged freely in sexual relationships with slaves, prostitutes, and *hetairai* (women—presumably mostly slaves who had bought their freedom—who had achieved a degree of education and cultural sophistication and seemed to have established longer-term relationships with one, or a small number of, men). Men also engaged in sexual relationships with younger males as part of these young men's initiation into adulthood and citizenship, although sexual relationships between adult men invited scorn.

Married women were kept under tight control in order to ensure that offspring were legitimate. Legitimacy became particularly important after Athenian citizenship was restricted to men who could show that both parents were Athenians. Because women's sexual appetites were also acknowledged and often exaggerated, the possibility of women evading the prohibition of sexual activity outside of marriage was a source of anxiety for their husbands. A woman who wished to be seen as "above suspicion" had to work hard not to invite any hint of impropriety.

meeting, in which she persuades Lichas, who has brought Iole to Trachis, to tell her the truth about Iole's identity, Deianeira presents herself as a woman who understands the passion that has "sickened" Herakles and asserts that her understanding will allow her to tolerate Iole in her house. Minutes later, however, she admits she cannot do so. Her empathy for Iole and her self-presentation to Lichas as an understanding wife are not an act put on for the occasion, as the abruptness of the reversal in her attitude might suggest. They represent both her natural instinct to empathize and identify with other women and her knowledge of Herakles. She shows sophisticated intelligence when she understands what kind of self-presentation will persuade Lichas to trust her. But when she enters the house after this speech, she experiences physically what she is losing: not only her position in the household and her security but also the satisfaction of her own desire for Herakles.

Deianeira also understands that it is sexual power that has given her a secure place, not the characteristics she has just demonstrated with Iole and Lichas: intelligent self-reflection, an understanding of others, and persuasive eloquence. She sees her aging body next to Iole's young one, the two of them in the same bed waiting for Herakles, and she knows that she is powerless to preserve her world. Because the audience has experienced her humanity and the depth of her ability to express her own and Iole's condition, her reduction to a body no longer desired is felt (at least by some, we can imagine) as a loss. Through the dramatic revision of Deianeira's sense of herself—from the woman who pities Iole and speaks to Lichas with deep understanding of human nature to a helpless wife threatened unbearably by a sexual rival—Sophokles asks the audience to consider what this sudden, dramatic shift in Deianeira's attitude represents. If women are valued only in their role as sexual partners and producers of children and if women's security is contingent on these roles, does society risk losing the benefit of the kind of strength, intelligence, and humanity that Deianeira displays with Iole and Lichas? Does the audience experience that loss when they see her act only out of her insecurity and fear?

Then, in her powerlessness, Deianeira turns to magic, in antiquity a dubious practice—as she herself tells us. Magic is, at best, the last resort of those who are desperate and have no other resources and, at worst, a dangerous way to bend others to one's will by attempting to harness supernatural power. Sophokles does not dramatize Deianeira's mental and emotional struggle to decide to act in this way. When she returns to the stage, after she has applied the potion, she describes in detail to the chorus only the actions she took, not what she was thinking or how she was feeling. It is the fact of her taking action that matters, not her motivation. It seems that not acting is impossible in her desperate position, and magic, however dangerous, is the only action available to her to prevent her erasure.

Deianeira's potion was given to her by the Centaur, Nessos, who attacked her sexually as he was ferrying her across the river Evenos on her trip from her father's to Herakles' house. On hearing her cries, Herakles shot Nessos fatally with one of his arrows tipped with the poison of the Hydra of Lerna, whom he had killed during one of his labors. Nessos, as he was dying, instructed Deianeira to gather the blood in his wound and use it, whenever the need might arise, to win back Herakles' love. Critics have seen Deianeira as naïve in believing the Centaur; she herself asks, when she has realized that the potion will destroy Herakles, how she could have believed it was a love potion. Some argue that by her use of this potion, she must intend, consciously or subconsciously, to destroy Herakles, in revenge for his destruction of her world. But Sophokles does not reveal to the audience her frame of mind as she prepares the potion. Instead, her account focuses on the nature and limitations of her agency. It is her taking action that the audience sees through her description. By focusing on the steps of the action itself, then, Sophokles seems to suggest that if only covert, indirect, and wildly uncontrollable resources are available, then covert, indirect, and uncontrollable actions will result. In picturing Deianeira's action so vividly, he questions whether the passivity that society expects of women, their limited agency, is not just a diminution of their being but is also dangerous in its consequences. The circumstances, as Sophokles dramatizes them, are extreme, as we expect from tragedy. But the conditions they reveal can be transferred, without a great leap of the imagination, to the everyday lives of Athenian women.

When Deianeira learns from her son Hyllos the effect the potion has had on Herakles, she leaves the stage in silence, and the audience then hears from the Nurse an account of her suicide. The loss of Deianeira's voice places her beyond the audience's comprehension; she is no longer able to describe publicly her situation, as she has done throughout the play. This sudden remoteness, when she has been so present, is mitigated only by the Nurse's subsequent description of Deianeira's private world inside the house, as she touches the objects there, visits the hearths, which will now "be deserted," and recognizes the women who have shared that world with her. The Nurse allows the audience to follow Deianeira into this private world, onto her marriage bed, until the moment she exposes her body and takes hold of a sword. But like the silence that accompanies her final departure from the public space of the stage, the final action she takes in this private world cannot be narrated, as the Nurse does not witness it. It happens in complete isolation and in silence. Finally Deianeira recreates the conditions she has described to the chorus at the beginning of the play as the enclosed space of childhood, a place not open to intrusion. By stabbing herself with a sword on her marriage bed, she brings into vivid juxtaposition that safe and secure place and the male force—both Herakles' and Nessos'—that has destroyed it. Because the audience must recreate the scene in their imagination from the Nurse's description, they engage intensely with the circumstances of her death.

In what follows between Herakles and Hyllos, we see two men

facing, like the audience, what Deianeira has shown them. Hyllos, the Nurse tells us, enters her world both imaginatively and physically; he understands what has driven her to suicide, and he weeps for her, stretching out next to her, expressing his grief without the constraint men are expected to display. Herakles cannot. His reaction to the news of her death is to demand vengeance, and when he learns that the source of his destruction is Nessos' potion, he dismisses Deianeira entirely from his mind. Through these two men, the audience is offered two models for what to do with the unusual theatrical experience of being drawn imaginatively into the private, domestic world of women.

3. HERAKLES

The fact that Deianeira dies before the expected reunion with Herakles on his return dramatically underlines the distance between their worlds. When Herakles finally enters, what does the audience learn of his world, the male world? Herakles has been present throughout the play in the references to him made by Deianeira, Hyllos, Lichas, and particularly the chorus, and of course the audience will associate him with various stories and ritual practices. In the mythic tradition, he is a deeply ambiguous figure—a civilizing force who rids the world of monsters; a comic figure whose great strength is matched by his enormous appetites; a suffering man, hounded by the hatred of the goddess Hera, who drives him mad and leads him to kill his first family. His status as human or divine is also ambiguous. As the son of Zeus and a mortal woman, he both performs superhuman acts and experiences human suffering deeply. Upon his death, he is transformed by his father Zeus into a god. Athenians know him as a hero with a cult site, a figure who can offer protection to those who worship there, but also as a mythical character with human weaknesses. The audience cannot be sure which Herakles they will meet when he enters the stage, although earlier references describe him as "the best of men" (l.

243), celebrate his fame and his status as Zeus' son, and allude to his untiring exploits to benefit mankind. Yet Deianeira has also given a view of him as husband and father. In the first two-thirds of the play, then, there is ambiguity about which Herakles we will see.

Hyllos prepares us for the intense physical pain Herakles is suffering, and it is his pain that first dominates the stage, as he sings to convey its intensity and to plead for a quick death to stop it. Like Philoktetes in Sophokles' play of the same name, his body is pushed to the extreme of physical suffering, and he can only imagine death as a release from it. Whatever he has been, here he enters as a suffering man, whose whole being is focused on his body. When the pain subsides and he is able to speak, what dominates his thought is humiliation that his physical suffering is caused by a woman. This defeat and his weeping, which he says has turned him into a woman, are intolerable sources of shame, which he must erase by restoring his male identity. His attitude is closely aligned with central preoccupations of Athenian men: male strength and inviolability and an intense awareness of the way others view them. In the communal life of the Athenian citizen, a man's sense of his value rests largely in his ability to defend the city from her enemies with the strength of his body and to engage in the running of the city, a role that he can only fill effectively if he has the kind of reputation that lends authority to what he says in public fora.

When the pain returns, Herakles displays his body for all to see: what is now the site of his shameful suffering at the hand of a woman was once the instrument for all the labors he performed. By summoning witnesses and recalling his labors one by one, he restores the public view of his body as the source of his fame and his masculinity. Although the catalogue of his labors evokes his identity as a figure of myth, a hero and the son of Zeus, the audience may also recognize, in the association of his body with acts of strength, their own concerns for their reputation and the maintaining of their masculinity. His final act, he says, will be to bring order by imposing on Deianeira a just punishment and "compel[ling] evil to pay its due." Here again he presents himself in a way that conflates the mythic figure with the activities of an Athenian citizen ensuring the just order of the city.[6]

Herakles' pain and humiliation at being defeated by a woman and his determination to overcome that defeat establish the terms for an understanding of who he is in the play. He appears to be an embodiment of the agonistic Athenian male writ large and intertwined with the mythic hero. Just as we have seen the essence of the Athenian girl's and woman's experience dramatized in exaggerated terms in Deianeira's story, so in the figure of Herakles we see, on a grand scale, the pressures on the Athenian male to participate in the construction and protection of a just and ordered city and to maintain his reputation in a public role and as the male head of his family. While presenting the heroic Herakles on stage, Sophokles absorbs him, at least in part, into the exploration of gender that the first two-thirds of the play has developed. The figure hovers between the mythical Herakles, the recipient of a hero cult in Athens, and a contemporary Athenian male. The ambiguities of the one shadow the other.[7]

Herakles' dialogue with Hyllos grounds him more completely in this ambiguous position. When Hyllos is able to tell Herakles of

---

6. Every Athenian citizen was directly responsible for maintaining order in the city, whether by sitting on a jury, voting on legislation in the assembly, administering the day-to-day business of the city, or serving in the military. These activities helped to fashion how masculinity in Athens was defined. See https://www.atiner.gr/journals/humanities/2014-1-1-2-RUBARTH.pdf.

7. Hero cults very often center on a human figure whose life has blurred the boundaries both between god and man and between man and beast; the hero is both a superhuman and subhuman figure. In the myth of Oedipus, for example, he violates the most basic rules of civilized human behavior by killing his father and sleeping with his mother. Yet he became the focus of a hero cult and his grave, the site of his cult, was believed to give protection to the people who lived in its vicinity. By presenting Herakles, who was worshipped in a hero cult in Athens, both as a mythic figure and an Athenian citizen, Sophokles is able to associate the ambiguity of the hero as both a destructive and protective force with the Athenian male.

Nessos' role in his destruction, and of Deianeira's innocence and her death, Herakles sees himself restored to his mythic role as the destroyer of monsters. He can think of his defeat now as revenge from one of those monsters, not defeat by Deianeira, whom he erases from his thought and never mentions again. His confidence that this is Nessos' revenge is confirmed in his mind by an oracle he now reveals that predicted he would not die by the hand of a living being. It does not occur to him, as it may to members of the audience, that Deianeira also fits this description. Herakles now sees himself as a heroic figure defeated by one of his enemies. However, the oracle's possible reference to Deianeira, and Herakles' blindness to that possibility, allows the audience to see him also as a husband and father whose activity in the world and whose passions have brought destruction on his family and who remains intensely indifferent to that destruction. When he calls for his family to be summoned, Hyllos tells him that they have mostly dispersed to Tiryns and Thebes, underlining again the way in which the family as a cohesive unit is threatened by Herakles' role in the larger world, both as hero and as Athenian male.

These two ways of seeing Herakles meld into one when he demands that his son build him a funeral pyre and marry Iole. As the mythic Herakles, he is putting in motion the burning of his body on Mount Oita; Hyllos' refusal to light the pyre allows room for the tradition that it is Philoktetes (or his father) who does so and receives Herakles' bow in thanks. But as the head of the family, Herakles turns to its only remaining member, his son, to be sure that his funeral rites are properly performed and that he is given due recognition in death, so his name may live on. In his demand that Hyllos marry Iole, Herakles determines the union that, in myth, leads to the founding of the Heraclidae, the family from whom the Dorian kings claim descent. But as a father commanding his son to obey him, he is ensuring that the order of his shattered family is restored by securing a bride worthy of Hyllos' status as his son. By extending his erotic attachment to Iole beyond his death in the marriage of Hyllos and Iole, Herakles seeks a more extreme version of the immortality men imagine for themselves by leaving behind them a son to carry on the family line. Against Hyllos' moral abhorrence at Herakles' demands, Herakles asserts the primary demand of a father: to be obeyed. One of the fundamental rules that creates social order in Athens, that the male head of the family must be obeyed and the child must honor his parents, overwhelms Hyllos' resistance to performing what, to him, is close to parricide and incest. Hyllos' assent to Herakles' demands recognizes Herakles' position as the head of his family, but his unease about the nature of Herakles' demands may also lead the audience to think critically about the dangers inherent in such power.

Herakles' certainty about the meanings of the oracle may also lead the audience to wonder about the confidence he has in his own authority, since oracles are generally understood to give mortals only glimpses of divine knowledge and are notoriously difficult to interpret with certainty. He is sure that the oracle that says he will not be killed by a live being refers to Nessos; he doesn't even acknowledge the other possibility: Deianeira. Another oracle explicitly offers two possibilities: that the present moment will bring either a release from his labors or his death. He is certain that it predicts his death, and his certainty leads him to arrange that outcome. As he is a mortal man (his physical suffering and expectation of death lead the audience in this moment to see him as mortal), this claim of more-than-mortal knowledge of, and control over, the future, including his own death, may lead some to question the wisdom of such confidence. Moreover, his determination to act, and force Hyllos to act, on the basis of this understanding may seem, at best, a problematic assertion of his authority. Are members of the audience being led to shrink, as Hyllos does, from the unquestioning authority to impose his will that Herakles claims as a man and a father? As the son of Zeus and the hero who in contemporary Athens has a cult and receives worship, Herakles makes demands that are the natural culmination of the narrative of his life. But the audience also views him as a husband and father. His immediate dismissal of Deianeira as the agent of his defeat and of Hyllos' moral abhorrence of his demands, as well as the unquestioning confidence he has in his interpretation of two ambiguous oracles, may cause some to cast a critical eye on the standards of behavior for and the power afforded to the Athenian male within the family.

4. THE END OF THE PLAY

The ambiguity about Herakles' identity and how to view it reaches its most intense dramatization in the play's ending. Just as the narrative of his return brings with it the expectation, created by other such stories, of the meeting between husband and wife, so the dramatization of Herakles' final day brings with it, for some, the expectation of his apotheosis. *Women of Trachis* ends with his own and Hyllos' assumption that he is being carried to Mount Oita to die on the pyre Hyllos will build him. There is no explicit reference, however, to his transformation into a god by the intervention of Zeus, which other accounts of Herakles' life describe. Sophokles ends the play with deliberate abruptness, before Herakles' final hour. What is at stake in leaving it to the audience to imagine what will happen in his final moments? Are the final words—"in all this there is nothing / that is not Zeus"—an indication that Zeus will indeed care for his son, or is it a confirmation of Hyllos' judgment in the previous lines that the gods "look on / indifferent / to suffering like this"? And if it is left to the audience to imagine what will happen, what do these two choices mean for their understanding of what they have just witnessed on stage?

This question relates to the relationship between the first two-thirds of the play, which is dominated by Deianeira's presence, and the last third, in which the focus is on Herakles. If the audience takes seriously the intimate picture of a woman's life and its difficulties drawn by Deianeira's words and actions, and if her silence in response to Hyllos' accusation and the vivid picture of her suicide linger in their minds, then the question of Herakles' death or apotheosis must relate somehow to what the audience has experienced in the first two-thirds of the play for the play's structure to be coherent. If an audience member imagines at the end of the play that Herakles will die on the pyre and Zeus will remain indifferent, then his suffering and death balance Deianeira's; both stories are then the tragic result of the distance between them and their inability to share more than mutual destruction. And some might be led to wonder if men and women might find a way to share a life without destroying each other. Are a woman's dependence on the male and her lack of a sense of her own agency harmful to society? Do a man's power over his family and the expectations of him that come with his role both as head of the household and an agent in the affairs of the city blind him to the suffering of those without that power?

But some critics have seen Deianeira's role in the first two-thirds of the play simply as a way to give us an indirect picture of Herakles before he enters the stage and to build anticipation before his entrance. If Deianeira's story is subordinated in this way to Herakles' or the intensity of Herakles' presence displaces from the audience's mind Deianeira's story, then the ending may seem to be the final chapter of a life of more than human effort and triumph, and it would be more fitting to that view of the play to imagine that Zeus finally rewards his son with divinity in his final hour. And then the erasure of Deianeira's narrative, her silence, and her death dramatize not only the imbalance in the place of men and women in the social order but also an imbalance in the order of the universe: the power and dominance of the male universalized in the act of the father Zeus reaching down from Olympus to rescue and deify his son. Audience members, of course, may imagine both these possibilities and therefore be led to think about the different implications each has for the world in which they live.

5. THE FUTURE: IOLE AND HYLLOS

Both of these imagined endings have consequences for the two other characters left on stage at the end of the play: Hyllos and Iole. (The role of the chorus, who is also there, will be addressed later.) In our translation, Iole has emerged from the house and is addressed by the chorus at the end of the play. Although it is unusual for a character to enter the stage unannounced, it is also unusual for a silent character to be so central to the plot of the play. Since Iole never speaks, and since introductions of an entering character usually precede their speaking, it seems possible to imagine an unconventional entrance here. There is also much uncertainty about who speaks the final lines of the play and to whom they are addressed as well as precisely what is said (see the note to these lines in the translation). There is no sure answer to these questions. Here in particular a translator acts as interpreter. By choosing to have the chorus address Iole and tell her not to stay in the house but, by implication, join the final tableau of Hyllos carrying Herakles to Mount Oita, we are allowing the audience to imagine that Sophokles means to suggest the possibility of a different future for this younger generation.

Hyllos is the only character who interacts directly with both Herakles and Deianeira while each is on stage. He shows an understanding of, and sympathy towards, both his parents. He learns too late that his accusation of his mother was wrong, but we see him act on that new understanding in both the love he shows his mother's dead body and the resistance he offers to Herakles' condemnation of her. And, despite his horror at the thought of doing what Herakles asks of him, he accedes to his father's wishes by finding a compromise: he will build but not light the pyre, and he persuades himself that obedience to his father is a duty that should override his moral and emotional revulsion at the thought of marrying Iole. Hyllos, therefore, shows a depth of understanding of, and sensitivity to, both the male and female perspectives of the main characters. Does his new understanding open up a possibility that his and Iole's future relationship will be different from his parents'? This is an intriguing question in a play where, up to this point, understanding has only come to characters too late for them to act on it.

Iole's silence makes her a blank slate for the audience's imaginations to fill. Many may view silence as appropriate behavior for a woman in public, especially a slave as Iole now is. But the audience has heard what Deianeira has seen in her, a capacity to "understand her own feelings" (l. 442), and in the final lines, the chorus recognizes the enormity of what Iole has witnessed. Some may then imagine that her exposure to "great and strange" (l. 1759) deaths and "many sufferings / never heard of before" (ll. 1761–62) gives her the possibility of a different future, when they remember how Deianeira's inability to look at the battle between Herakles and Acheloos and her lack of experience in the world outside the house had limited her. There may also be a glimmer of a different possibility for Hyllos and Iole in the way Deianeira dies and Herakles suffers, especially if his suffering is seen as the prelude to his death on the pyre, not his apotheosis. Deianeira stabs herself like a man, and Herakles sees himself in his pain as a woman. Does that crossing into the other's world, even if only in death, open up the possibility of a different future for the next generation, a future that the audience can imagine and learn from? These are all questions raised by the enigmatic ending of the play. They have no definitive answers, but they are surely raised by an engaged viewing of the play's structure and interactions.

6. THE CHORUS

Another perspective on the divided male and female worlds of the play comes from the chorus, young unwed girls from the town of Trachis. Their perspective is, of necessity, different from the characters in the play because as a chorus they do not engage in the play's action: the Chorus Leader speaks to the actors, almost exclusively Deianeira and the Nurse, in the episodes, but as a chorus, they sing and dance; they do not act.[8] In their character as young women, they are closely aligned with Deianeira's world; in fact, they do not sing after Herakles has entered the stage. And yet Deianeira recognizes that the young, unmarried women cannot understand her situation, as they have no experience of their

---

8. The structure of all extant Greek tragedies involves the alternation between episodes involving three speaking characters (wearing masks so that no play requires more than three male actors to play the various characters) and the songs of a chorus. The chorus representing young women of Trachis is played by twelve or fifteen male citizens (depending on a play's date earlier or later in the fifth century BCE) whose participation in the chorus is part of their civic training and responsibility. One member of the chorus acts as its leader and speaks the lines given the chorus in the episodes. As with the actors, chorus members wear masks and may represent old or young people, men or women, slaves or citizens. Although the chorus has a character—in this play, young women of Trachis—the members of the chorus differ from the actors in a number of ways, even beyond their presence as a group rather than as individuals.

The contrast between the actors and the chorus is established by several stylistic and dramatic conventions. First, the actors speak; the chorus dances and sings. While the entire play is written in verse rhythms, the rhythm used in the episodes is iambic trimeter, a meter the Greeks considered the closest thing to the rhythms of everyday speech. The chorus sings (and dances) in a variety of complex rhythms that are associated with verse written for other kinds of occasions and choral performances associated with a number of different rituals. Second, by dramatic convention, choruses do not participate directly in the action of the play. The clearest example of this enforced inaction happens in Aeschylus' *Agamemnon* when the chorus of male citizens are hearing the sounds of Agamemnon, their king, being murdered inside the house and, standing at the door of the house, ask one another what they can do, instead of rushing in and stopping the murder. Their point of view on the action of the play is therefore different from the actors, who have to make decisions, take actions, and assume responsibility for the consequences of those actions.

The contrast between chorus and actors is therefore visible, audible, and substantive. It is not possible to generalize across playwrights or even plays what the role of the chorus is. But clearly the differences in the modes of performance of actors and chorus require that a reader or viewer of a Greek tragedy not expect the chorus's role to be simply another character on the stage.

own that would allow them to enter fully into her feelings and thoughts. Therefore, both as characters and as performers, they are removed from the world of the actors. That distance becomes vividly clear in their lengthiest exchange with Deianeira, when she appeals to them for support and reassurance in her use of the potion to secure her position with Herakles. The Chorus Leader's response to her question (ll. 838–48) could not be more equivocal. At the moment when Deianeira makes her crucial choice to act, the chorus does not participate.

What perspective, then, does the chorus bring to the events of the play? It is in their songs and the accompanying dance that the lives of Herakles and Deianeira are brought together into a whole. All of the chorus's songs include both Herakles and Deianeira as their subject. Because the rhythms of the songs are repeated in each pair of stanzas, a stanza with Herakles as its subject will often have the same rhythmic structure as a stanza focusing on Deianeira. And because each song is a coherent and isolated unit in the moment of its performance, each song gives their stories, as the song is performed, an ordered unity that is absent in the action of the play, in which consequences are carried forward from scene to scene. The unity each song creates for Deianeira's and Herakles' stories—a unity the characters cannot achieve—depends on the nature of the chorus's performance: the sound of their song, the form of their dance.

Their songs make frequent reference to the sounds and movements they are making as they perform; these references to their mode of performance draw attention to how song and dance transform Herakles' and Deianeira's stories. The songs, which have the formal structures of hymn or song of healing (paian) or prayer, mediate between the human world and the divine order. They suggest the possibility that humans can give shape to their world not—or not only—by trying to take an action but by creating a moment and a movement outside of the temporal sequence of cause and effect that the action entails. In that moment, as they dance and sing, their voices and movements create a repeated pattern that incorporates Herakles' and Deianeira's stories in the larger divine order to which their song gives expression and appeals. Sophokles thus juxtaposes the unsuccessful attempt of the characters to bring order to their world by their actions and the chorus's ability to suggest a different way to view that world. Their point of view, however, which is already by the nature of its performance different from the characters', is harder to imagine as a resource for the characters' situation as the play progresses.

The content of the chorus's songs moves from hope for the reunion of Herakles and Deianeira to sorrow for the pain the characters suffer and finally a wish to disappear, just before Herakles' entrance. In this progression, their way of representing the events and feelings Deianeira and Herakles struggle with seems further and further removed from the actuality of that struggle. The height of their hope comes in their fourth song (ll. 902–40), when they pray for Herakles' return "full of desire" for Deianeira, the effect, they imagine, of the gift she has sent. The song occurs just before Hyllos enters to tell of the devastating effect of the potion on Herakles' body. The dramatically ironic juxtaposition of their hopeful prayer and Hyllos' devastating account makes vivid the contrast between their vision and the characters' experience of the events unfolding on stage. In the next song, they sing of the awful truth of the oracle that predicted Herakles' "release" from his labors and of Deianeira's unknowing participation in bringing it to pass. Their grief for what has happened is connected to their sense that the events are part of a larger order, predicted by the oracle, beyond the characters' understanding or control. The pain they sing of at the end of the song is disembodied—"A stream of tears / pours out spills over: / the sickness spreads" (ll. 1195–97)—and they name Aphrodite as "the doer of these deeds" (l. 1211). The absence of a sense of human agency and the movement in the song from the suffering of particular people to a kind of universal pain are countered in the very next scene, when the audience learns of Deianeira's suicide.

Deianeira has acted in response to the circumstances the chorus has just described, asserting her agency in contrast to the absence of human agency in the chorus's song. Finally, just before Herakles' entrance, their last song expresses the wish to be removed entirely from the sight of Herakles "bound in pain he can't escape" (l. 1330); after Herakles' entrance, the chorus falls silent. Their wish cannot be fulfilled, of course, because by the conventions of the theatre, the chorus does not exit before the end of the play. But their wish and the silence that follows illustrate dramatically the limit in their ability to address the action as it unfolds. In this brief summary of the relation of the chorus's song to the actions of the play, it is perhaps possible to see how the perspective this chorus of young women offers seems inadequate to the circumstances of the moment in which the play is happening. But perhaps, like Iole and Hyllos, their songs also suggest a future that might be more receptive to their vision.

In the parodos, the first song (ll. 132–95), the chorus urges Deianeira to have hope by giving form in the imagery and, presumably, the sound and movement of their song and dance to the constant flux of human existence, a vision that counters her pessimistic belief in her life's consistently downward spiral. Using the imagery of the sea and the stars, they make the perpetual cycle of rise and fall, suffering and joy, vividly present on stage. This attitude of hope arises out of a vision of balance and constancy in the rhythms of life, which the movements of their dance may also reflect. Similarly, the song creates a balance between Herakles' and Deianeira's points of view, containing them both in a coherent whole. For the audience, this vision may seem, as we've seen, more and more deluded in the face of what happens on stage. Their hope in an ordered world with the gods as its overseers, where Herakles' and Deianeira's stories are also united and balanced, may be sustained only by the nature of song and dance themselves. Because song and dance are part of a continuous and repeated tradition of formal or ritual occasions, at some time in the future, another chorus may sing a song that shares this chorus's vision of the world, and perhaps then the songs will address more persuasively the circumstances of those who hear it. The chorus's belief in ordered change and their performance, in which rhythmic dance and sound enact the nature of such change, provide the basis for such a future, in contrast to the more and more destructive actions of the characters in the episodes between their songs.

We can illustrate how the songs the chorus sings may evoke a future more receptive to their vision by looking more closely at two of them. At the height of Deianeira's distress, when she has learned what Iole's presence really means, the chorus, alone on stage for the first time, sings a song narrating the battle between Herakles and Acheloos that Deianeira has talked about in her first speech. The song (ll. 700–758) is vivid in its descriptions of the combatants, the sounds and movements of their battle, and the situation of Deianeira, alone and apart, awaiting the outcome, especially if one imagines their movement in some way representing the battle they describe. Hearing and seeing it, the audience is taken back to a time in the past at the very moment in the play when Herakles' present desire is about to destroy the life he and Deianeira have created as a result of that former battle. The song gives an ordered rhythm to the violence of male erotic desire, and it brings into that picture, with the same rhythms and movements, the solitary world apart of the young bride. It preserves the distance between the male and female worlds while finding a form to contain them both just when, in the action on stage, the presence of Iole brings these worlds into fatal contact. And it evokes Aphrodite as the "referee," the divine presence who is both within and above the fray, the ultimate ordering power. The audience may take hope from the way this song gives form to a past erotic struggle; the song allows them to imagine that the chaotic and fatal struggle now unfolding between Deianeira, Herakles, and Iole also may find, in the future, an equally ordered retelling.

In the next song (ll. 902–40), as the chorus awaits Herakles' return after Lichas' departure with Deianeira's gift, they attach the joy of his return to the very sound of their song: "soon the lovely sound of the *aulos* / will rise to you once more . . ." (ll. 910–11). The song is a prayer for his return in triumph, full of desire for Deianeira, "seduced by that beast's beguilement," although its appeal, in which many gods are mentioned, is not addressed to a particular god, as hymns of prayer usually are. It seems it is the song itself that will bring him home through its sounds and rhythms and urgent expectation. There is, of course, irony in the discordance between their prayer and what, we soon learn, will be the reality of Herakles' return. Their hope is, it seems, cruelly undercut by the action that is about to unfold. But, as one scholar has argued, this song may also be a projection into the future, beyond the time of the play's present, into a time when Herakles' apotheosis on Mount Oita will be celebrated in a festival that enacts his annual return.[9] With a few textual changes, the song would, word by word, work as the hymn sung at this festival. But even if we don't accept these changes, the song may strike the audience as a ritual hymn of this sort and may thereby have an effect with its own power and promise, despite the action about to take place. Song as part of a repeated ritual transforms a moment rooted in the temporal framework of human experience into a constant present, in which humans participate in, and gain strength and hope from, a larger order. Perhaps, then, although the chorus is silenced by Herakles' entrance, the hope that their song and dance have offered remains a possibility in the performance of songs in the future, in which the audience themselves may participate.

Or perhaps the chorus's final expression of grief and their subsequent silence through the last third of the play are another way that Sophokles engages the audience in feeling the cost of the deep division between the male and female worlds. In the last song, the

---

9. Margalit Finkelberg, "The Second Stasimon of the 'Trachiniae' and Heracles' Festival on Mt. Oeta," *Mnemosyne* 49.2, 1996, 129-43.

young women of Trachis picture the grief and loss at the heart of Deianeira's and Herakles' stories:

> What first to wail—what woe?
> And what, after that, what woe?
> Hard in my misery to know.
>
> The things within now we all see
> and what's to come we wait to see—
> now and future all one. (ll. 1318–23)

Does their silence through the last third of the play challenge the audience to keep alive in their memory this song, which unites Deianeira's and Herakles' pain and collapses the past, present, future into the one moment of its expression? Just as Deianeira's silence at the end challenges the audience to carry her story forward in their memory, so the chorus's silence after this song asks the audience to keep in their memory this expression of shared suffering, as they watch the final scene with Herakles, who now is the one who sings, and sings only of his own pain. This brief final song, in particular, has rhymes and rhythmic features that make it unique and memorable. And if the sounds of the chorus's songs echo in the audience's ears even beyond the end of the play, some might be led to think about the suffering caused by the imbalance in the roles of men and women and to hope for a different, less painful future.

7. CONCLUSION

The play leaves the audience to struggle with the many questions Herakles and Deianeira's relationship raises about both the way their society has constructed the roles of men and women and what possibility humans have to shape their world in the presence of divine power.[10] The Chorus Leader, in our translation, speaks the last lines of the play: "And in all this there's nothing / that is not Zeus." In addition to mentions of Zeus as the father of Herakles (who is most conscious of his father's absence, not his presence; ll. 1381–83), this claim to Zeus' overarching presence is most immediately felt throughout the play in the references to the oracles he has given Herakles, both of them puzzling riddles. The oldest, which we only learn of late in the play, states that Herakles will not die at the hand of a living being. The more recent oracle seemingly offers two possibilities for Herakles' life at the moment the play takes place: that he will be free of his labors, or he will end his life. On the most fundamental level, these oracles mark the distance between divine omniscience and the limit of human knowledge. They remind the audience throughout the play of the way humans

---

10. Attendance at performances of tragedies in the Festival of Dionysos in Athens played an important role in educating Athenians about their responsibilities as citizens. The playwrights were called teachers, not only because they taught the choruses the songs they were to perform but also because, more generally, the plays they wrote instructed the audience. Tragedy undoubtedly aroused strong emotions in the audience. But the circumstances of the performance—the open air, the lack of lighting and scenery to enhance the illusion, the size of the theatre, and the physical distance of large parts of the audience from the stage, for example—also meant that the audience could examine those feelings critically.

The three playwrights whose plays survive (Sophokles, Aeschylus, and Euripides) each found different ways to provoke the audience not only to feel but also to think. Sophokles' plays offer no straightforward answers to the questions they pose. The audience must struggle to find ways to resolve in their own minds the plays' tensions and conflicts. And although set in the mythical past, the plots of the plays focus on issues of importance for citizens of Athens to think about. Therefore, in thinking about, discussing with others, and arguing about the problems the plays pose but do not resolve, the members of the audience are engaged in educating themselves. No single interpretation of his plays will ever exhaust their ambiguities and interpretive challenges. For further reading about the role of tragedy in educating citizens, see https://research.duke.edu/5-questions-theater%E2%80%99s-role-democracy; http://www.leussein.eurom.it/democracy-and-the-ancient-greek-theatre/.

come too late to an understanding of the full meaning of their own and others' actions. They also seem to reinforce, in their riddling obscurity, the claim Hyllos makes at the end that the gods "look on / indifferent / to suffering like this." This indifference is mirrored in the chorus's songs, in the image of Aphrodite as a referee standing above and judging the fight between Acheloos and Herakles and as the "silent overseer" (l. 1208) and "doer of these deeds" (l. 1211), looking down on Herakles, Deianeira, and Iole as they suffer the consequences of her power.

Are then the gods' power and indifference the only divine manifestations that humans experience? Is the release from human suffering only possible through death, as Herakles decides is the meaning of the riddling oracle? Or do we heed the chorus's claim in the first ode that no one has ever seen Zeus "be careless / of his own children" (ll. 194–95) and do we imagine that Herakles, at least, will experience Zeus' saving hand? And can we experience that hope as any kind of consolation, given the imbalance it seems to create between Deianeira and Herakles and between men and heroes? In the bleak divide between men and women and between gods and humans that the play dramatizes, perhaps it is Deianeira's pessimistic assumption about the downward spiral of her life with which the audience can most completely empathize by the end of the play.

And yet if members of the audience can at the end understand and relate to that feeling of pessimism, their association with Deianeira's powerlessness and her lack of any sense of security is a source of future possibility, as are the chorus's songs. Perhaps the audience, like Hyllos who sees clearly the suffering of both his father and his mother, has not learned too late how to face not only the indifference of powerful gods but also the indifference of powerful men. Perhaps some may find a way to act on the understanding they have gained from being able to feel with those who suffer from that indifference.

SOPHOKLES'

WOMEN OF TRACHIS

Translated by Rachel Kitzinger and Eamon Grennan

WOMEN OF TRACHIS

[At the back of the stage stands the house where Deianeira and Herakles have been living in Trachis. One of the two other entrances onto the stage is from the direction of the town; the other is in the direction of Mount Oita, a mountain sacred to Zeus near Trachis.]

Deianeira enters from the house, followed by Nurse who stands aside. Deianeira speaks to the audience.

(Asterisks at particular lines indicate a note in the Notes section.)

Deianeira

You've all heard the old saying: I
There's no knowing a man's life—
has it been good? has it been bad?—
till he's dead.   *
But I'm not dead
and I can say *now*
my life is unhappy. It's a burden to me.
Listen.

When I was young
still living in my father's house—   10
Oineus' house, in Pleuron—   *
I shuddered with fear more than any girl in Aitolia
at the thought of marriage. Why?
My suitor was a *river*, the river Acheloos!   *
A shape-shifting monster!
He came to ask for me from my father:
one minute he was a sleek-shouldered bull;
the next—all twists and turns—a shimmering snake;
then a man-body with the face of an ox,
clear water gushing from his bushy beard.   20
At the thought of marrying him
I felt nothing but misery, and I prayed I'd die
before I'd have to lie in his bed.
For a long time he wooed me like that.
Then, at last, I was released:
the renowned son of Zeus and Alkmene   *
came to our house, and I welcomed him,
and he wrestled my river-suitor and set me free.
I can't describe the battle between them.
Someone who watched without flinching   30
could do that . . .
I saw nothing, knew nothing.
I just sat in a trance—
terrified my beauty would be my grief.
But Zeus ordains the end of every battle,
and this one he brought to a happy end . . .
if in truth it *was* happy.
For ever since he chose me as his bride
and made me partner in his bed,
I've felt fear, fear for Herakles.   40
One night brings trouble, the next drives it out,
only to bring more trouble in its place.

Yes, we did have children.
But—like a farmer who only visits some
distant field of his,
once at seeding time, once at harvest—
he'd see them only once in a while.
For the life he lived
had him always coming and going, leaving, returning—
always in service to one man or another.   50
And now, just when he's done with all *those* labors,
now I feel more worry, more dread than ever.
You see . . .
after he'd killed Iphitos,   *
we all had to move here to Trachis
and make our home in a stranger's house.
[turns to Nurse]
But then he left again! Who knows for where?
All I know is he left—and left me
to suffer bitter pangs for him.
I'm almost certain he's in trouble.   60
Ten . . . no . . . *fifteen* months he's been gone.
Without a word!
What else could it be but some catastrophe?
[She shows the Nurse a letter in the form of a scroll.]   *
When he left, he left this message.
I'm sure that's what it's about.
He gave it, and I took it.
But again and again I pray to the gods
taking it doesn't mean more pain.

Nurse   *

Mistress Deianeira, I've seen you so often
weep heart-scalding tears   70
each time Herakles headed off

on yet another labor.
But this time—if a slave's thoughts
may counsel one who's free—
I have to say something.
How is it, with so many sons,
you don't send one of them to look for your husband?
Especially Hyllos:
reason says he's best suited for the task,
if he's got any feeling at all for his father's name,   80
his glowing reputation.

[Enter Hyllos from the direction of the town, running towards the palace.]

But look, here he is, and just in time!
Dashing back like that to the house!
If you think I'm right,
do make use of him, and of my words too.

[Deianeira calls to Hyllos. She manages to divert his attention from whatever he was hurrying to do.]

Deianeira

Hyllos! Son!

[He comes to her.]

I've just learned that even someone lowborn
can be lucky and speak good sense.
Slave as she is, this woman here   *
has said what a free person might.   90

Hyllos

Can you tell me what she said, Mother?

Deianeira

She says that with your father gone so long
—and given his reputation—
you shame us [**he stares, perplexed**]
by not trying to find out where he is.

Hyllos

But I know already—
if I can trust the stories I hear.

Deianeira

You've heard where he is?

Hyllos

They say he's been a slave all this year.
Owned by a Lydian woman, ploughing her fields.   100*

Deianeira

Well, if he could put up with *that*,
we can believe anything.

Hyllos

But now he's freed from that at least.
Or so I'm told.

Deianeira

So where do they say he's living now?
Or is he lying dead somewhere?

Hyllos

In Euboia they say,
attacking Eurytos' city—or about to.

Deianeira

The city of Eurytos!
Did you know he left prophecies with me   110
about that very place? Ones we can trust.

Hyllos

What prophecies, Mother?
This is new to me.

Deianeira

That either he'll die there or—
once he's survived this last contest—
the rest of his life will be happy.
So now, with his future so much in the balance,
go and help him, child, won't you?
Either he's saved his own life—so we're safe too—
or else we all go down together.   120

Hyllos

I'll go, Mother. Of course I will.
I'd have been with him long ago

if I'd known of these prophesies.
But the lucky shape of Father's life
never let us fear for his safety,
nor worry too much for him.
Knowing what I know now, though,
I'll do all I can to find out what's happened to him.

Deianeira

Go then, my son.
Even if you learn good news late,   130
it can still be to your advantage.

[Hyllos exits in the direction of the town; the Nurse returns into the
house. Deianeira watches and listens as the chorus of young women
enters from the direction of the town, dancing and singing.]

CHORUS   ❊

O you whom shimmering Night
brings forth from her plundered womb
and day's end lays to blazing rest—
you, Sun, you I call to:
where is Alkmene's son?
Where is he?
Enlighten me now
you who blaze in flares of light.
Eastwards is it by the Black Sea straits,   140
or there, there
where two land-masses meet in the west.
Is it there he rests
from his heavy labors?
Say O Sun—
yours the strongest sight of all.

For I hear much-fought-over Deianeira
her heart full of yearning
cannot—like a trapped wing-flapping bird—
lay to sleep her eyes' longing   150
and cease her weeping.
Forever fresh is the fear she nurses
never forgetting
(her marriage bed bereft)
the road her husband travels.
That heavy weight wears away her spirit
always expecting the hurtful worst.

Just as a man might see
wave after wave
roused by a big wind north or south   160
rise and fall,
fall and rise
on the wide ocean:
so a sea of trouble
like that rough sea ever circling Krete
casts down then raises up Theban Herakles.   *
But some god or other
always hauls the unwavering man
back from the dark house of Death.

Since you see, Lady, only the wrong   170
in the way things are,
I must with respect
offer you another thought:
hold to the hope of some good outcome.
Zeus, son of Kronos,
the king who settles everything
sends no mortal a life without pain:
for pain and joy

come and go
go and come   180
turn and turn about
like the roundabout path of the Great Bear.   *

For not shimmering night,
not wealth, not mortal calamity
stays still for anyone:
but all of a sudden
grief or joy
comes to one, runs from another—
the one rejoices
the other mourns his loss.   190
So you too, royal Lady,
must cling to hope:
Who has ever seen Zeus
be careless
of his own children?

Deianeira

You've come—I imagine—because you've learned of my trouble.
May you never know through your own suffering
the agony destroying me.
Now you know nothing of it:
All young things are fostered in a place of their own   200
where no wind, no rain, no burning sun
disturbs them; there they grow
free of trouble, full of delight.
The life of a young girl is just like that
until that moment when, instead of *girl*,
she's called *woman*
and bears a woman's share of worry in the night:
fear for her husband or for her children.

Only then—
a woman with her own trials—   210
can she know the troubles that weigh me down.
Yes, I've shed tears over many things
but let me speak now of one thing
that's never happened before.
[She looks at the scroll she holds in her hand.]
When Herakles was last leaving home
he left behind this scroll with a cryptic message—
something he'd never dared talk about
when he left on his other labors.
Those times he'd leave like a man
setting off on a mission   220
not as one about to die.
But this time—
as if he were soon to leave this world—
he told me what property I should take
as my marriage portion and how his ancestral lands
should be divided among his sons.
And he said that when he'd been gone
a year and three months
then he'd either die or
should he survive beyond that time   230
he'd live out his whole life free from pain.
This, he insisted, was the end
the gods had set for all his labors.
And this, he said,
was what Dodona's ancient oak had uttered
through its two prophetic Doves.   *
And now—that time is here.
This is what's coming. Nothing can stop it.
It must end as it was foretold.
And so, friends,   240
I wake in terror from balm-sweet sleep,

full of dread that I must go on now,
bereft of the best of men.

Chorus Leader

Quiet now! There's a man approaching.
That garland he wears, it's a sign of good news.

[An old country man enters, the Messenger, from the direction of the town.]

Messenger

Lady Deianeira, let me be first
with the news that will lighten your dread.
Know he lives! The son of Alkmene lives!
He has prevailed, and takes
from the spoils of battle   250
offerings for the gods of the land.

Deianeira

What *story* is this, old man?

Messenger

Your longed-for husband—a man much envied—
will soon be here,
here at your house, and seen
as the conquering hero he truly is.

Deianeira

Who told you this? Citizen or stranger?

Messenger

The herald Lichas   *
tells this story to a crowd of men
in the meadow over there   260
where oxen graze in summer.
Soon as I heard him, I came straight here,
so I might be first with the news,
to win your gratitude . . . and be rewarded.

Deianeira

And Lichas, why—if his luck is good—
why is he not here himself?

Messenger

He's not at ease there, my Lady,
surrounded by all the men of Malis,   *
who hold him there with their questions.
Each one has his own question, wants his own answer   270
and won't let go till he's satisfied.
So—against his will and bending to theirs—
Lichas remains there with them.
But he'll be here soon, and you'll see him.

Deianeira

Oh Zeus, you who hold dominion
in the unploughed meadow of Mount Oita,
you have given me—though after so long—
given me joy. Women, raise your voices—
you within the house and you outside—
for a vision rises from this report   280
bright beyond hope, and we rejoice.

CHORUS

Let the house all shout
cries of joy: ululations
sung at the hearth
of this house that soon
will celebrate a marriage!

And let the men too
raise together
their chant to Apollo
the great Protector,   290
his quiver bright-shining.

All together girls
girls all together,
lift a loud paian, your paian   ❋
to Artemis his sister
torch-bearer
born on Ortygia   ❋
huntress of deer
and to the Nymphs
always beside her.   300

Now I rise up:
nor will I be deaf
to the *aulos*, the *aulos*   ❋
master of my heart!

Euoi   ❋
how it shakes me—
Euoi euoi!—
the ivy! the ivy

in its bacchic whirl!
Io io—Paian the Healer!　　　　　　　　310

Dear woman now see
a sight so clear
shining right here
before your eyes.

[Lichas enters from the direction of the town; a group of bedraggled-looking women follow behind him.]

Deianeira

Yes, I see it, dear women.
I'm all eyes; I haven't missed it.
And though he's been a long time coming,
I bid this herald welcome.
[Deianeira turns to Lichas.]
Welcome indeed,
if you bring welcome news.　　　　　　　　320

Lichas

Yes, Lady, our coming is good indeed,
as your welcome, too, is fitting
for all that's been accomplished.
It's only right a man's success
should reap a harvest of good words.

Deianeira

Dearest of men, tell me first my first desire:
Will I welcome Herakles home alive?

Lichas

So, at least, I left him: strong, thriving, full of life;
not sick nor slowed by any wound.

Deianeira

Where? Here—in this land—   330
or in a stranger's country?

Lichas

He's on a promontory in Euboia,
marking sites for altars
and choosing offerings to Zeus of Kenaia: *
the spoils of war due to the god.

Deianeira

So vows he made will be fulfilled?
Or is it because of some prophecy?

Lichas

Because of certain vows he made, yes—
when by sheer force of his spear
he was sacking the land of these women.   340

**[He gestures to the group of women behind him. Deianeira walks
over and looks at each of them, then turns to Lichas.]**

Deianeira

These women . . . in god's name . . . who *are* they?
Whose are they?

They seem—unless their misfortunes deceive me—
to deserve our pity.

Lichas

He took them, my Lady,
when he plundered the city of Eurytos.
He chose them . . . for . . . himself . . .
And . . . as a gift for the gods.

Deianeira

Was it to attack *this* city he was gone
for days beyond counting?   350

Lichas

No. Most of the time—as he says himself—
he was detained in Lydia. Not—so he says—
as a free man but sold into service.
You mustn't resent this account, Lady,
for it seems Zeus was responsible.
Herakles was sold to Omphale, a foreign queen,
and served her—he says so—for a full year.
And this bitter insult so soured him
he took an oath and swore to himself
that—no matter what—he'd enslave   360
the man who had caused this suffering,
and enslave too his wife and child.
And it was not a vain vow:
for when he was free again
and rid of the stain of slavery,
he raised a fighting force of mercenaries
and laid siege to the city of Eurytos.

Because he claimed that of all mortal men
only *he* was responsible for what he'd suffered.
How so?   370
Well, when Herakles had come as a guest
to his hearth—come as an old friend and ally—
Eurytos slandered him in talk,
abused him with malicious intent,
declared that in any contest of archery—
even though Herakles' quiver
was brimful of arrows that never miss—
he'd be left in the dust by Eurytos' own sons.
And on top of that he called him "slavish boor!"
Then, at a feast, when Herakles had drunk too much,   380
Eurytos threw him out of his house.
Of course Herakles was enraged, and so,
when Iphitos, Eurytos' son, came some time later
to the hills of Tiryns
in search of his straying horses,
Herakles took him by surprise there:
when Iphitos was looking
one way with his eyes, another with his mind,
Herakles hurled him down from
the summit of a towering cliff.   390
That enraged Lord Zeus—Olympian Zeus,
Father of all—so he sent Herakles
to be sold into slavery. The god, you see,
would not tolerate this deed.
For, alone of his victims, Herakles
killed Iphitos with trickery.
Had he defended himself openly,
Zeus would have looked on with sympathy,
since Herakles would then have acted justly.
For not even the gods take kindly   400
to violent abuse, which is why

those brazen-tongued men of Oichalia
are all now in Hades and their city enslaved.

And so these women you see before you, my Lady,
have exchanged a life of prosperity
for a life no man could envy
and come to you like this.
This is what your husband commanded.
And I, in all loyalty, fulfill his command.

He himself—when he's made offerings   410
to his father Zeus for the sacking of that city—
he will come, be sure of it. And *this*—
among all the good things I have spoken—
this must be sweetest to your ears.

Chorus Leader

Now, Queen: because of what you see
and all you've learned from this herald,
here is joy, joy bright-shining.

Deianeira

Of course his words gladden my heart.
Of course I rejoice at my husband's success.
Of course my feelings must match his deed.   420
But if one thinks at all, it's only natural
to worry for a man who enjoys success, worry
one time or another he may trip and fall:
just look at these poor women.
The sight of them fills me with pity.
Strangers in a strange land,

homeless wanderers without fathers.
Once, no doubt, the daughters of free men.
Now they must live a life of slavery.
Oh Zeus, lord of the turning tides of battle,   430
may I never see you turn on *my* children like this,
and, if ever you *do*, may I never live to see it.
That's the fear I feel when I see these women.
[She looks at Iole and walks over to her.]
And *you*, poor girl, who are you?
Are you unmarried? Are you a mother?
By your appearance, it seems all this
is new to you; it seems you're nobly born.
Lichas, whose daughter is she?
Who is her mother? Who the father?
Tell me—who gave her life?   440
For, of all these women, her I pity most—
She alone seems to understand her own feelings.

Lichas [dismissively]

What do *I* know? Why ask *me*?
It's possible her family is . . .
not among the lowest there.

Deianeira

Is it possible she's from the ruling family?
Does Eurytos have a child?

Lichas [interrupting]

I don't know.
Truth is, I didn't ask many questions.

Deianeira

Not even her name?   450
Wouldn't one of these women have told you?

Lichas

That least of all!
I did what I had to do in silence.

Deianeira [turns to Iole]

Then, poor girl, tell me yourself.
It pains me not to know who you are.

Lichas

She won't loosen her tongue—
not if she stays as she's been.
Since we started out, she's revealed nothing.
Nothing big, nothing small. Nothing.
Since she left behind her wind-swept homeland,   460
she's been weeping: crushed, poor thing, under her misfortune.
I know it's a bad state she's fallen into,
but it asks for tolerance and understanding.

Deianeira

Leave her be, then.
Let her enter the house as she wishes.
Let me not add to her misfortunes.
She's borne enough already.
Now let us all go in—
[to Lichas] You may go wherever you need to.
I will take care of what's needed in the house.   470

[Lichas and the captured women move towards the house. The Messenger, who has been listening to Lichas with bemusement, signals to Deianeira, moving between her and the departing women.]

Messenger

Lady, first linger a little here alone.
Let the others go in as you've directed.
You may learn then
who it is you take into your house.
I know what you need to know,
what you haven't heard yet.
I know . . . everything!

Deianeira

What's this about? Why stop me like this?

Messenger

Stay and listen to me.
What I told you before wasn't useless, was it?   480
What I say now won't be either, or so I believe.

Deianeira

Should we call those women back again?
Or do you want to speak to me
and these women here [**gesturing to the chorus**]?

Messenger

I'll speak to you and these women.
Let the others stay where they are.

Deianeira

Well, they're gone now. Tell your story.

Messenger

In what he said to you just now, this man
didn't speak straight, nor tell the whole truth.
Either he's wrong now,   490
or he was, earlier, no honest reporter of what he knew.

Deianeira

What do you mean?
I don't understand you.
Tell me what you're thinking. Be clear.

Messenger

I myself heard this man, Lichas,
say before many witnesses
that Herakles seized Eurytos and high-towered Oichalia
just to have that young girl
[pointing to the door that Iole has now entered].
Then, Lichas said, Eros—Eros alone of the gods—
bewitched him into launching that attack.   500
It wasn't what happened in Lydia,
nor his slavish servitude to Omphale,
nor hurling Iphitos to his death.
Just now, though, for you here
this man changed his whole story:
he simply wiped Eros out of it.

Fact is, when Herakles couldn't persuade Eurytos
to give him his daughter for his secret pleasure,

he gives some petty excuse as his motive,
then attacks her homeland and sacks her city.   510
And now, as you see, he's on his way home
and has sent her to this house deliberately—
not as a slave. Oh no, Lady, don't imagine that!
Is that likely—is it—if he's burning with desire?

I thought it only right, Mistress, to reveal
all I happened to learn from that herald.
And a great many men of Trachis
—in the middle of the agora there—
[gestures to the entrance in the direction of the town]
heard what I heard. They can provide proof.
What I say may not warm your heart . . .   520
I'm sorry for that. But
I've spoken nothing but the truth.

Deianeira [to herself]

Oiy . . . misery! What's happening to me?
What suffering have I brought under my roof,
not knowing what I was doing?
Oh my grief! Unhappiest of women!
[to the Messenger]
Is she nameless then, as he swore,
that man who brought her here into this house?
This girl whose beauty is a burning flame,
whose very presence shines like the sun?   530

Messenger

She was the daughter of Eurytos.
Iole was her name.
Lichas, of course, couldn't tell you that
since, as he said, he "asked no questions."

Chorus Leader

May evildoers be destroyed—
especially those who lie
whose job it is to speak the truth.

Deianeira

Women, what can I do? I cannot speak.
This story roaring in my ears,
it strikes me dumb.   540

Chorus Leader

Go to Lichas.
Perhaps if you questioned him with force—
interrogated him—he'd give a clear account.

Deianeira

You're right. Yes. I'll go.

Messenger

Should I wait here? What should I do?

Deianeira

No, stay!
[Deianeira points to Lichas, as he enters from the house.]
Look, he's quitting the house without my summoning him.

Lichas

I'm going, Lady. What should I tell Herakles?
Instruct me. I'm leaving right now.

Deianeira

Oh how you rush off!   550
And you were so slow in coming.
Now you're going before . . .
before we can continue our talk.

Lichas

True, but if you want to ask me something,
here I am, at your service.

Deianeira

But are you to be trusted?
Will you tell me the truth?

Lichas

As great Zeus is my witness!
At least about such things as I know.

Deianeira

Well then—   560
who is that woman you brought here?

Lichas

A woman of Euboia.
Of what family I can't say.

[The Messenger interrupts.]

Messenger

You! Look at me!
Who do you think you're talking to?

Lichas

And what do *you* mean by asking such a question?

Messenger

Answer, if you've any wit at all!

Lichas

To Queen Deianeira, if my eyes don't deceive me.
Daughter of Oineus, wife to Herakles, and my mistress.

Messenger

Just what I wanted to hear.   570
So this woman *is* your mistress?

Lichas

She is, and rightly so.

Messenger

Well then, if that's the case, what penalty
should you pay for not doing right by her?

Lichas

How not right? What are you hinting at?

Messenger

No hints, no hidden meanings.
You're the master of *that*.

Lichas

I'm going. I was a fool to listen so long.

Messenger

No. Not before you've answered one little question.

Lichas

Ask away. It's clear you're not going to be quiet.   580

Messenger

That captive woman you led into the house . . .
you know the one I mean?

Lichas

I do. Your point?

Messenger

Didn't you say before that she was Iole,
Eurytos' daughter? The one you brought here
but now look at as if you didn't know her?

Lichas

To whom did I say such a thing?
Who will swear it?
Where will he come from?

Messenger

From the town. Many will swear it. A great crowd   590
heard you say it in the agora of Trachis.

Lichas

Yes . . . well . . . they *claimed* to hear.
But there's a difference
between reporting an *impression*
and giving an accurate account.

Messenger

What *impression*? Didn't you speak under oath?
Didn't you say
you were bringing that young woman here,
as wife to Herakles?

Lichas

His wife? Dear Mistress, by all the gods—   600
who *is* this fellow?

Messenger

One who was there, and heard you say
it was *desire*—desire for Iole—
caused that city's destruction.
It wasn't the Lydian queen did that, but eros—
the passion of Herakles—obvious to all.

Lichas

Mistress, bid this fellow stand aside.
Argue with a lunatic!
Who in his right mind would do that?

Deianeira

I beg you in the name of Zeus   610
who flings the lightning bolt
across the high valleys of Mount Oita:
don't deceive me by hiding this story.
It's not a spiteful, craven woman
you tell your tale to, no, nor to one
ignorant of the human condition:
I know it's not in our nature
for the same things always to keep us happy,
nor for the same people to be happy always.
So whoever—like a boxer with raised fists—   620
stands up against Eros is a fool.
Eros bends even the gods to his will,
and he does me too.
So why not another woman like me?
I am mad indeed if I fault my husband
when he's in the grip of this sickness.
Or fault this woman who, along with him,

has done nothing shameful, no wrong
against me. No, it's not like that.
But if Herakles taught you to lie,   630
you've not been well instructed.
And if you taught yourself this lesson,
you will simply look bad when you want to look good.

Come now, tell me the whole truth.
If a free man is called a liar,
he'll never outlive the shame of it.
And if you think you won't be found out,
you're wrong:
many men heard you tell your story
and they'll tell me everything.   640
But if it's fear you're feeling,
you've no reason for that.
It's *not* knowing that would hurt me.
What's so terrible about knowing?
Hasn't Herakles—just one man—slept with many other women?
And not one of them has ever heard—
at least not from me—
a bad word. Not one word of reproach.
Nor would this woman,
even if he should melt away   650
with love for her. Because the truth is
I felt great pity for her when I first saw her.
Her beauty has wrecked her life
and—ill-fated as she is—
she has, against her will,
destroyed and enslaved her own homeland.
But let all this go, blow away on the wind.
What I'm telling you is
you may do hurt to someone else,
but to me you must never lie.   660

Chorus Leader

She speaks good sense. Listen to her.
If you do, you'll have no reason
to find fault with her later.
And from me you'll earn thanks.

Lichas

Dear Mistress,
now I will tell you the whole truth,
since now I know you're a woman of sense—
a mortal woman who is of this world.
I'll hide nothing. It's as he says.

Not long back a ferocious passion for this girl   670
pierced Herakles through and through.
Because of her
with his spear he overthrew then sacked
her father's city, Oichalia.
But I must speak, too, on his behalf:
he never told me to conceal all this,
nor ever denied it. On my own, Mistress,
I spoke those words; I on my own made that mistake—
if indeed you see it as a mistake:
I did it to shield your heart from hurt.   680

And now—
since at last you know the whole story—
now do what's good for you
and at the same time good for him.
Good for both of you.
Put up with this girl. Stay true
to those words you spoke about her.

Keep in mind that in all else
the strength of Herakles prevails,
but in *this*—in his passion for this girl—   690
he was utterly undone.

Deianeira

So, we are of one mind in this.
I'll do as you say. I will not sicken myself
in a losing battle against the gods.
Come, let's go in, so you can take with you
a message for Herakles. Gifts too,
to match those you arrived with.
You came leading a rich procession
and shouldn't leave here empty-handed.

[Messenger exits to the town; Lichas and Deianeira go into the
house.]

CHORUS

A mighty force   700
ever-victorious
is Kypris Aphrodite.   *
Her dealings with the gods
I pass over
and won't repeat
how she tricked
the son of Kronos
night-shrouded Hades
earth-shaker Poseidon.
But who were they   710
who came seeking
this girl as a bride?

Who were they
contended as rivals
struck blow after blow
dust choking the air?

On one side the river
big-horned bull-powerful
all bulging muscle:
Acheloos of Oiniadai.   720*
On the other side
from Bacchic Thebes   *
stood the son of Zeus
high-brandishing
his tightened bow
his club his spear.
To the center they came
clashing together
yearning for her bed.
And there too alone   730
at the heart of the fray
Kypris Aphrodite
who blesses the marriage bed
and in her hand
the staff of judgment.

Then there sounded
the loud clamor of battle—
blows arrows bull's horns
clanging together.
Strangleholds with death-dealing   740
smashing of foreheads:
loud groans
from both combatants.

But apart on a hillside
bright in the distance
the girl in her beauty
sat and waited
for the one who would mate her.
Like a mother   *
I show you her face: 750
the bride-to-be
the one they fought for.
She sits alone (*oh pity her!*)
awaiting the outcome.
And like a young heifer
suddenly astray
she's far from her mother
alone, all alone.

[Deianeira enters, carrying a wooden casket.]

Deianeira

While Lichas is in the house
bidding farewell to the captive girls,   760
I've come out, unseen, to tell you
what I've contrived with my own hands.
And also what I suffer—for I need your comfort.

I've taken into my house a girl—
no, no longer, I think, an innocent girl,
but a woman with experience of men.
Like a merchant seaman taking on cargo
I've taken in this freight that abuses my heart.
And now we two women under the same blanket
wait for one embrace.   770
Day after day I've kept his house for him

and he repays me with this? Herakles?
The man they say is trustworthy and good?
But I can't be angry with him,
stricken as he is with this disease.
But then . . . live in the same house with her?
How could I? What woman could?
Share the same bed, the same man?

I see her youth,
how alive it is, while mine is fading.   780
A man's eye loves to seize
the flower in bloom
but turns away from the dying blossom.
So here's what I fear: that they'll call
Herakles my husband but this girl's lover.

But I've said it before: it isn't good
for a sensible woman to nurse her anger.
So let me tell you the way I've found
to free myself from pain.
Long ago   790
I received from Nessos, an ancient Centaur,   *
a gift hidden now in a vessel of bronze.
I was still a young girl when I got it
from the shaggy-breasted beast as he lay dying.
With my own hands
I drew it from his mortal wound.

He used to carry men for a fee
across the deep waters of the Evenos.   *
He didn't row or sail them over
but carried them in his arms.   800
Me, too, he bore on his shoulders,
when I followed Herakles the first time—

sent by my father as his wife.
But, in the middle of the river,
Nessos touches me lewdly with his hands.
I cry out.
At once the son of Zeus swings round
and with *his* hands he sends an arrow
whizzing through the Centaur's shaggy breast
into his lungs.   810
As he lay dying, the beast said to me:
"Child of old Oineus,
since you are the last I carried across,
you will benefit this much
from my ferrying—if you obey me:
take with your hands
the clotted blood from around my wound
—where my blood is dyed black
by the arrow's poison
once drawn from the Hydra of Lerna.   820*
And this will be a charm over Herakles' heart:
no woman instead of you,
when he lays eyes on her,
will he ever love more."

I thought just now of this gift
(well-hidden since Nessos died)
and I've used it to dye this tunic.
I rubbed it in exactly as he told me
before he died. And now it's ready.

May I never learn—nor even consider—   830
wrong, reckless acts: I hate women who do.
But if somehow with this potion,
these spells over Herakles,

I might prevail over this girl,
then I've made it ready—
but if it seems I act too rashly
I'll stop right now. [**She puts down the casket.**]

Chorus Leader

Well, if there is reason
to be confident about such actions,
it seems to us your plan's not a bad one.   840

Deianeira

I'm confident enough
to *think* my plan will work,
but I haven't yet *tested* it.

Chorus Leader

Well, if you act you must know.   ✳
Even if you've reason to think it will work,
you wouldn't be secure
without putting it to the test.

Deianeira

We'll know soon enough. [**Deianeira picks up the casket.**]
I see Lichas at the door. He'll be away in no time.
Only, please, shelter me with your silence.   850
Even if one does something
that puts honor at risk,
one won't sink in the world's esteem
if it's done in darkness.

[Lichas enters from the house.]

Lichas

What are your orders, child of Oineus?
Tell me. I'm already late.

Deianeira

Yes, I've been getting things ready for you, Lichas,
while you were inside speaking to the strangers.
So now you may take this tunic
woven by my own hands: take it with you   860
to Herakles, a gift to him from me. **[Deianeira gives him the casket.]**
And when you give it to him, make clear
no man must put it on or have it touch his skin
before *he* does. The light of the sun
must not see it, nor any fire blazing
on any hearth or in any sacred precinct—
not till my husband stands revealed
and displays it to the gods on that day
he slaughters bulls for them in the open air.
For I made this vow: 870
if ever I should see him
back safe in this house,
or hear for certain of his return,
I would dress him in this tunic
and show him shining to the gods:
a new celebrant in new raiment.
And take with you, as a sign of this vow,
something my husband will know right away:
the wax impression of my signet ring.
[She seals the casket with wax and her signet ring.]
So now be on your way,   880

and remember a messenger's first rule:
never meddle. Make sure
my gratitude to you is added to his,
so one favor becomes two.

Lichas

I will. If I'm well practiced
in the art of the messenger—the craft of Hermes—   *
I won't fail you; I'll carry this casket
and deliver it just as it is.
And I'll add to it, as guarantee,
the words you've spoken.   890

Deianeira

Please go now. You understand
how things are in this house.
You know the state of it.

Lichas

Yes, I know, and will say all is well.

Deianeira

And you know too—you saw it yourself—
how I received the foreign girl with kindness.

Lichas

Yes. I was amazed and pleased—
a heart-warming sight.

Deianeira

So then, what else could you say?
[**to herself as he leaves**]
Though I'm afraid you may speak too soon of my longing for him,   900
before you know if he desires me too.

[**Lichas leaves in the direction of the town. Deianeira exits into the house.**]

CHORUS

O you who live
by those ship-harboring inlets
and the warm springs running
from the rocky crags of Mount Oita
and by the mountain-surrounded Bay of Malis
and by the shore
sacred to Artemis of the golden shaft
the Gates where assemblies of Greeks grew famous: *

Soon the lovely sound of the *aulos*   910*
will rise to you once more—not harsh not doleful
but like the Muse's heavenly lyre:
for the son of Zeus and Alkmene hurries home
carrying trophies his courage has won!

Away for a year
abroad on the sea
while we waited here
enduring his absence
knowing nothing
while his unhappy wife   920

forever shedding tears
wore away her heart.
But now Ares aroused
brought release
from days of labor.

May he come!
May he come!
May his many-oared ship
bear him on and not stop
till he reaches this town.   930
May he leave the hearth
on the island over there—
where they say
he offers sacrifice.
May he come lightly
come full of desire
seduced
by that beast's beguilement
seeped into his shirt:
bewitching persuasion.   940

[Enter Deianeira from the house in agitation.]

Deianeira

Oh women, what have I just done?
I fear it's gone too far!

Chorus Leader

What is it, Deianeira, child of Oineus?

Deianeira

I'm not yet certain, but I despair
when I think the good I hoped to do
will soon be seen as a great wrong.

Chorus Leader

Is it your gift to Herakles?

Deianeira

Yes. I'd never advise anyone now
to rush eagerly—blindly—into any action.

Chorus Leader

Tell us, if you can, why you're afraid.   950

Deianeira

Because something's happened
that will shock and astonish you.
The thing I used just now to anoint the tunic—
a scrap of woolly fleece from a white sheep—
it's vanished!
Not eaten up by anything in the house!
It devoured itself!
It wasted away into little shreds
spilling over the edge of the rock where I left it.
Here's the whole story, exactly what happened.   960

What that beast, the Centaur, long ago
—in agony from the bitter barb in his side—

told me to do, I did.
I followed every instruction, left nothing out,
as if his words were inscribed on bronze,
impossible to erase.
Here's what he told me and here's what I did:
I kept this potion deep within the house.
It was not to be exposed to fire,
nor warmed by the sun, nor touched   970
till I was ready to rub it on something.
I followed these instructions exactly.
But now, needing to act,
I rubbed it on the tunic with a tuft of wool
plucked from one of our sheep.
In the house, in my room, in secret I did it.
Then—out of sight of the sun—I folded the gift
and placed it in the casket I showed you.

But just now, when I went outside, I see something
impossible to put into words or understand.   980
I happen to toss that tuft of wool
into a beam of sunlight, and as it grows warm
it starts to flow, it loses its shape.
Then it crumbles into the earth—
like something you'd see a saw spew out
from a length of wood it was cutting.
It was just lying there, where it had fallen,
when from the earth beneath it
clots of foam came frothing up—
like the foam of the rich wine   990
fermented from the gray-blue grapes
of Dionysos' vine when poured onto the earth.   *

So now I'm in agony; I don't know what to think.
But I see I've done something awful.

For why in the world would the dying beast
have offered *me* a kindness?
Wasn't *I* the reason he was dying?
It's not possible. No. He bewitched me
because he wanted to destroy *him*—
the one who wounded him.   1000
I'm coming to understand this too late
when it's no longer of any use.
For, if I'm not deceived, I alone—
oh, misery—will destroy him.
I know this now. That same arrow
that struck Nessos
caused great harm even to the god Chiron.   *
Whatever monster it touches it destroys—
destroys every one of them.
How will it not destroy Herakles too,   1010
that poison seeping from the beast he wounded,
that black poison mingled with his blood?
This at least is what I think.
And so it is decided: the same blow
that fells him will strike me down too.
For if a woman who puts being good
above all else hears people speak ill of her,
she cannot bear to live.

Chorus Leader

Of course you're terrified
to see such strange, such frightening things.   1020
But you mustn't be too hasty
to judge their outcome.

Deianeira

But the plan I made was no good.
Now nothing can reassure me or give me hope.

Chorus Leader

But the anger of others is softened towards those
who in all innocence have stumbled and fallen.
And so it should be for you.

Deianeira

A woman who's helped create a disaster
could never say that. You may say it,
because you're not burdened by troubles of your own.   1030

[Enter Hyllos from the direction of the town, agitated.]

Chorus Leader

Better keep quiet now; say no more—
unless you want your son to hear you.
He's here.

Hyllos

Oh Mother . . .
would I could choose one of three things:
either that you were no longer alive;
or, if you were,
that someone else would call you "Mother."

Or that you could swap your heart and mind
for a better mind, a better heart.   1040

Deianeira

What have I done, child, to make you hate me?

Hyllos

My father—your husband—you've killed him!

Deianeira

[**cry of horror**] What is it you're telling me, child?
What story is this?

Hyllos

A story that has to find its end.
If something comes into the light of day,
nothing can make it not be there.

Deianeira

What do you mean, child?
Who told you this story:
that I have done a deed I could never want?   1050

Hyllos

No one told me, I saw it with my own eyes.
My father's monstrous misfortune!

Deianeira

Where did you come near him?
Where was it you stood by my husband's side?

Hyllos

If you must know, here's the whole story.
Having sacked the famous city of Eurytos,
Herakles marched on, hauling with him
the spoils of victory: the enemy's weapons
and the best of all they took from the city.
There is a sea-washed headland in Euboia—   1060
Cape Kenaion—where he marked off altars
and a tree-shaded sacred space
to his father Zeus. There I saw him first,
and my longing turned to joy.

As he's about to perform his rich sacrifice,
his herald Lichas arrives from home
bearing your gift—the fatal tunic.
Having put it on exactly as you instructed,
he sets about slaughtering twelve bulls.
Perfect they were, the prize beasts of the spoils.   1070
He intended to sacrifice a hundred beasts in all,
cattle and sheep all mixed together.

At first, poor man, he was
in a good mood as he prayed,
enjoying the tunic with its glittering ornaments.
But as the flames
from the pinesap and the sacrificial victims
flared bloodred,
sweat beads stood out on his skin—and the shirt

clings to his sides, fixed there 1080
as if by a carpenter's hand—mantling every joint.
A biting spasm then shook his bones
and a deadly poison—as if from some
vicious serpent—began to feast on him.
Then he shouted at poor Lichas—a man
in no way responsible for the bad *you'd* done:
"What cunning plan is this, to bring me this tunic?"
Then ill-fated Lichas—who knew nothing—
replied it was your gift, yours alone,
just as you'd sent it. When Herakles heard this 1090
and another spasm
shot through him, throttled his lungs, he grabs Lichas
by the foot—just at the anklebone—
and hurls him against a sea-washed rock.
White scraps of brain splatter his hair,
his skull splinters, blood sprays out.

Then from the crowd—from the awed silence
that descended—a great wail rose,
a cry of grief for the one wracked by pain,
the other smashed to bits. 1100
No one dared go near Herakles.
His convulsions flung him shouting and shrieking,
down to the ground, up into the air.
The surrounding rocks echoed with his cries—
the hilly headlands of Lokris,
the rocky shore of Euboia—
till the poor man grew exhausted
from flinging himself on the earth
and from his howling cries.
Again and again he cried out 1110
at the ruinous union with you—wretched woman!—

and the marriage alliance with Oineus
that had ruined his life.

Then looking up from the murk of smoke,
his eyes rolling back in his head, he saw me
in the crowd, tears flowing fast from my eyes.
Holding me in his gaze, he calls out to me:
"Son, come! Don't run from my catastrophe—
not even if you must die with me.
Lift me up, take me away.   1120
Best, take me where no man will see me.
But at least—if you have any pity in you—
take me from this place! Now, right now!
Do not let me die here!"
These were his commands.
So we put him in a boat, sailed him here.
No easy task—with the roaring he made
each time a spasm convulsed him.
But any moment now you'll see him—
still alive or, in these last moments, dead.   1130

This, Mother, is what you've plotted
against my father. This your guilty act.
May the Fury and avenging Justice make you pay—   *
if it's right for me to pray for that.
And it *is* right:
you yourself have given me the right
by killing the greatest man on earth—
a man like no other you'll ever see.

[Deianeira starts to exit into the house without speaking; the Chorus
Leader calls after her.]

Chorus Leader

Why do you leave in silence?
Don't you know your silence accuses you,   1140
just as *he* does?

[She keeps going without any response and exits into the house.]

Hyllos

Let her go!
May a fair wind take her out of my sight!
Why should I tend the dignity of the name "mother"
if she does nothing a mother would?
Let her go! Good riddance! Farewell!
May the joy she's given my father
be hers too!

[Hyllos exits into the house to ready a bed for Herakles.]

CHORUS

See, friends,
How sudden it's upon us: 1150
the gods' prediction
long ago foretold!

It said
when twelve ploughing seasons
had come and gone
in the same number of years
the yoke of his labors
would then be lifted
from Zeus' own son.

And so—sure as a vessel   1160
come to port in fair wind—
it's come to pass.
For how could a man
who sees light no longer
still bend though dead
beneath the load
of his labors?

For if the Centaur's deadly web of deceit
clings vise-like to his sides
while the stinging poison   1170
death-spawned and born of a shimmering serpent
seeps into his skin,
how could this man live
to see the light beyond today?
The soot-haired Centaur's
lying words cast killing darts
piercing him all over—
his flesh bubbles and bursts.
How then can he live?

And none of this   1180
she feared, this misery-ridden woman,
when she saw the huge harm
of a new marriage
rushing headlong at her house
and tried herself to remedy it.
But through a fatal exchange
the false mind of another
played its part too.
And, see, she laments,
and sheds in despair   1190
the dew of her tears.

And the coming doom reveals
the awful ruin
of that deceit.

A stream of tears
pours out spills over:
the sickness spreads.
[cry of despair]
No suffering so piteous
was ever inflicted
never by enemies   1200
on his famous body.
[cry of despair]
You dark spear point
in the van of battle!
Swiftly you bore her
with the thrust of your spear-tip
the new-made bride
from high Oichalia.
And the silent overseer
—*Kypris Aphrodite!*—
is revealed: 1210
the doer of these deeds.

[A cry comes from within the house.]

Chorus Leader

Am I wrong? or is that
a piteous cry from the house?
That wailing? Someone crying out.
A cry of anguish.
Something terrible is happening!

[Enter Nurse from the house.]
Do you see this old woman?
Her downcast face! Her clouded brow!
She's come to tell us something.

Nurse

Oh girls, that gift sent to Herakles   1220
kindled no small calamity.

Chorus Leader

What's happened, old woman?
What are you saying?

Nurse

Without taking a step
Deianeira has made her last journey.

Chorus Leader

Surely not dead?

Nurse

       Yes.

Chorus Leader

She's dead?

Nurse

       Again yes!

Chorus Leader

Poor miserable woman, how did she die?

Nurse

A cruel deed!

CHORUS [singing] ✻

Tell us . . . oh tell us
what death did she meet?   1230

Nurse [speaking]

Run through by a double-edged sword . . .

CHORUS [singing]

What impulse what illness
cut her down
with the dark point of that terrible weapon?
How did she contrive this other death—
death piled on death?
How, being alone, did she find a way?
One cut
from the sorrow-steeped blade?
Are you sure?   1240
Did you see this violent act?

Nurse [speaking]

I saw it. I was right there.

CHORUS [singing]

Who did it?
Tell us.

Nurse [speaking]

She, by herself, with her own hands.

CHORUS [singing]

What do you mean?

Nurse [speaking]

It's plain as day.

CHORUS [singing]

That new-made bride has given birth
and brought forth a great Fury
in this house!   1250

Nurse

True. And had you been beside her
and seen what she did,
you'd have pitied her all the more.

Chorus Leader

But could a woman's hand
dare such a deed?

Nurse

Yes, it could, strange as it seems.
Hear me now:
you can be witnesses to what I've seen.

When she went alone into the house
and in the courtyard saw her son   1260
readying a soft-matted bier to take to his father,
she hid herself where no one could see her,
in the women's quarters.
There she fell wailing before the altars
crying out they'd all be deserted now.
And she wept, poor woman, as one by one
she touched those simple things
she'd always used around the house.
Now here, now there
she wandered through the rooms   1270
and if she saw anyone—any maid or servant
dear to her—she'd burst into tears at the sight of them.
In despair she cried out for her own fate
and for the household hearths
left empty now forever.

When she'd done with her lament,
I see her rush into Herakles' bed-chamber.
Still hidden in the shadows,
I see her throw covers on her husband's bed
and spread them out. Then she throws herself   1280
upon them, in the middle of the bed,
and weeping hot tears, cries out:
"Oh bed, oh my marriage: Farewell!
Farewell now forever. Never
will you welcome me, his bedfellow, again."

That was all she said. Then with urgent hand
she loosens her robe, undoing the gold pin
that fastens it above her breast,
and bares her left side and left arm.
I ran then, fast as I could,   1290
to tell her son what she intended.
But in the time I raced there and back,
she stabbed herself with the two-edged sword   *
through her side, her liver, her stomach.
Her son, when he saw her, cried out in anguish.
He knew, poor thing,
that in his anger he'd driven her to this.
He had learned, you see—too late—
from people in the house
that she'd done what she did   1300
without meaning to,
led on by that beast, the Centaur.

Then the poor boy could not stop
weeping and lamenting over her,
couldn't stop kissing her.
Stretched out by her side, he lay beside her
and groaned again and again
that he'd hurled accusations
—empty, awful accusations—at her.
And he wept aloud   1310
that now he'd lose both of them
and have to live alone—with no father, no mother.

That's how it is now within the house.
And that man who thinks he can reckon on life
for two days—let alone more—is a fool.
For there is no tomorrow
till you've survived today.

[Nurse exits into the house.]

CHORUS

What first to wail—what woe?
And what, after that, what woe?
Hard in my misery to know.   1320

The things within now we all see
and what's to come we wait to see—
now and future all one.

Would a favoring breeze would blow,
blow by the house
and take me away—
so I won't die of fear
the moment I see
Zeus' great hero-son bound for the house
bound in pain he can't escape.   1330
Oh, unspeakable sight!

[A procession of men accompanied by a doctor enters from the direction of the town, carrying Herakles on a bier.]

Near he was near
when I keened for him now
like a nightingale
with mournful clear voice.
And now here it is—
this procession of strangers.
How do they bear him?
As if a loved one.

Each silent heavy step   1340
laden with care.
Aiiiii, the silence!
He makes no sound.
What should we think?
Dead?
Or has sleep overcome him?

[Hyllos enters from the house and runs up to the approaching procession.]

Hyllos [chanting]   *

[**cry of grief**]
I weep for you, Father, for your suffering I weep.
[**another cry of grief**]
What's to become of me? What will I do?

Doctor [chanting]

Quiet, child! Don't waken
the wild pain raging   1350
in your fury-minded father.
He's barely alive. Be quiet. Bite your tongue. . . .

Hyllos [chanting]

                      What are you saying, old man?
Is he alive?

Doctor [chanting]

Don't wake him, he's sunk in sleep.
Don't rouse the rabid sickness that strikes him,

again and again strikes him.
Child, don't excite it.

Hyllos [chanting, more frantic]

But a great weight crushes me.
This misery drives me mad.

Herakles [chanting]

Oh Zeus! Where am I? Who are these people?   1360
I'm tortured by this relentless pain!
[cry of pain]
Such agony eating me alive!
Monstrous, abominable!
[groan]

Doctor [to Hyllos, chanting]

Now see how it's best to be quiet?
Not chase sleep
from his eyes, his mind?

Hyllos [chanting]

Yes, but to do so is not in me.
At the sight of such horror
I can't hold my tongue.

    Herakles [singing]   *

   O, altars I built on rocky Kenaia!   1370
   Would I'd never laid eyes on you!
     Ah misery!
   What return you've earned me

for the sacrifices I made—such sacrifices!
What misery! Zeus!
What humiliation, what outrage
to feel this madness blossom
no spell can mend!

What magic, what medicine, what physician
will repair this ruin?   1380
None but Zeus.
It would be a wonder to see him
even far off.
[Hyllos tries to ease his father's torment.]
EE . . .
Leave me! Let me sleep! Leave me be!
Doomed! In torment!
Where do you touch me?
How lay me down?
You'll kill me, kill me!
You've wakened what was sleeping!
It tightens its grip.   1390
This thing comes again!
[cry of pain]
Who are you, you Greeks! Most unjust!
For you I destroyed myself   *
cleansing your seas, clearing your forests
of all that was bad in them.
And now
will no one bring fire or lift a sword
to relieve my pain?
EE . . . **[writhing on the ground]**
Will no one come—no one—
to strike off my head?   1400
To free me, release me from this loathed life?
[cry of despair]

Doctor [chanting, as he stoops to try to calm Herakles]

Son of Herakles,
this calls for stronger hands than mine.
Help me.

Hyllos [chanting, as he cradles Herakles' head]

I lay my hands on him,
but there's nowhere . . . no way . . .
to give him a life without pain.
That is in the hands of Zeus.

Herakles [singing]

My son, where are you?
Take hold of me here.   1410
Raise me up! [**cry of pain**] Oh god!
Again it springs at me, leaps to destroy me—
this abominable thing.
This vicious sickness no one can heal.
Io io Athena! Again
this savage thing tears me to bits.
Oh my son! Pity your creator!
Draw your innocent sword!
Strike this head from my shoulders!
Heal this agony   1420
your godless mother has caused
driving me to rage!
Oh may I see *her* writhing on the ground like *me*,
like *me* may *she* be destroyed.
Come Death, come sweet Death!
Brother of Zeus,
lay me to rest, to rest!

End my misery,
swift-winged Death.

Chorus Leader

Friends, I shudder when I hear the king   1430
suffer like this.
Such a man struck by such disaster!

**[Herakles, the pain abating, raises himself to a near-sitting position
with the doctor and Hyllos on either side of him.]**

Herakles

Ah! Many are the labors hot and hard
—hard even to speak of—
I've done with my hands, my broad back.
But not even Zeus' wife or hated Eurystheus   *
ever subjected me to the like of this:
this woven net of Furies   *
Oineus' two-faced daughter
has tangled me in.   1440
Fast-grappled to my sides, it eats away
every last layer of flesh:
destroys me, dwells in me, drains my lungs
of every moist breath, has drunk up already
my fresh-flowing blood.
Fettered by this monstrous shackle
my body wastes away to nothing.
No battlefield spears, no army of earthborn Giants;
no strength of savage beast; no land at all—
not Greece, not any foreign land, not anywhere   1450
I came and cleansed of monsters—
ever did this to me. It was a *woman*—

no *manly* woman, no sword in her hand—
a woman alone who has overthrown me.
[**Herakles takes hold of Hyllos' wrist.**]
My son, be a true-born son to your *father*,
don't respect more the name of *mother*.
With your own hands take her from the house.
Bring her here to me, the mother who bore you.
Give her into my hands. Then I may be sure
the sight of my ruined body makes you   1460
grieve more for me than you'll grieve for her
when she suffers at this righteous hand.
[**Hyllos gets up and moves away, agitated at what he is hearing.**]
Come, son! Be bold! Pity me! I deserve pity!
I who weep and wail like a girl.
No one can say they've ever seen me like this.
Even in the grip of disaster
I never as much as whimpered.
But now, for a thing like this—*this!*—
I become a woman in all men's eyes.

Come close now. Stand here by your father.   1470
Look, look at this racked body.
Off with these coverings. [**He tears them off.**]
Behold, all of you, this miserable body!
My wretchedness . . . see! . . . the pity of it!
[**Herakles cries out in pain.**]
This lacerating spasm sets fire to me, pierces every pore.
This desperate, brute, devouring disease
gives me no peace, no rest!
            Ah, Lord Hades, take me in!
            Strike me, bolt of Zeus!
            Lord, send it down!   1480
Father, cast your thunderbolt!
Now this thing feasts on me again;
like a flower blossoming, it bursts open inside me.

O hands, hands, back, shoulders, chest . . . O beloved arms!
You limbs that once conquered
the lion of Nemea, scourge of herdsmen,
a beast unassailable, unapproachable,
subdued it with your strength!
And the Hydra of Lerna.
And the double-natured galloping man-horses   1490*
—a ferocious host of them—
lawless, violent, strong beyond measure.
The Erymanthian beast too,
and the monster offspring of dread Echidna,   *
that three-headed mastiff of Hades
none can do battle with.
And the serpent-guard of the golden apples
at the end of the world.
Other labors too—thousands of them!
And no one ever set a trophy up   1500
in triumph over me.
                        But now this, this!
All disjointed, torn to bits, I lie in ruins—
overthrown by a destroyer I cannot see.
I, child of a peerless mother,
I the son of Zeus who lives among the stars.
But, if nothing else, be sure of this:
even if I'm nothing, even if I cannot move a limb,
I will, even as I am,
lay my hands on the woman who did this.
Only let her come!   1510
I'll teach her so she'll tell the world
that I—alive or dead—I
compel *evil* to pay its due.

[He falls silent.]

Chorus Leader

Alas, poor Greece!
On the horizon I see only grief
when she is left without this man.

Hyllos

Your silence, Father, gives me leave to answer you,
and though you're ill, listen to me please.
I will ask for what is right, what is just.
Give yourself over to me.   1520
Let go the anger that gnaws at you.
If you don't, you cannot learn
how empty it is,
the satisfaction you desire,
and empty too
the very source of your grievance.

Herakles

Say what you have to say, then be silent.
I'm sick. I understand nothing.
What have you been hinting at all this time?

Hyllos

I will speak of my mother.   1530
I will explain the state she's in now
and those mistakes she made in ignorance.

Herakles

Vile thing! Again, in my hearing,
you speak of *her*, your father-murdering mother!!?

Hyllos

Yes, her. Given her state now,
it's not right to stay silent.

Herakles

Indeed it's not—
given the wrong she's done already!

Hyllos

And not—even you will say—
given what she's done today.   1540

Herakles

Speak! But be careful:
don't show yourself a vile traitor.

Hyllos

I will speak.
She's dead. Killed. Just now.

[Herakles pauses for a moment.]

Herakles

A weird thing your dark words have prophesied.
Who did it?

Hyllos

She herself. No one else.

Herakles

[cry of anger]

Before she could die by *my* hand, as she should?

Hyllos

Your fury—even *that*—would fade
if you knew everything.   1550

Herakles

A strange way to start.
Say what you mean.

Hyllos

Here's the whole story:
She had intended to do good
but was mistaken, completely mistaken.

Herakles

Good!? Vile boy!
Good!? To kill your father?

Hyllos

It was a love charm she intended to give you
when she saw your new bride beneath her roof,
but all went wrong.   1560

Herakles

And who is so powerful a sorcerer
among the men of Trachis?

Hyllos

No. It was Nessos the Centaur.
Long ago he persuaded her
she could—with this potion—
arouse wild desire in you.

[Herakles is silent for a moment, then utters a cry of despair.]

Herakles

Oh unhappy! Long-suffering! I'm destroyed!
Mine no longer the light of day.
[cry of despair]
I see clearly now where I stand in the scheme of things.
From this moment you have no father.   1570
Go, child.
Summon all my children, your brothers and sisters,
and summon poor Alkmene,
whose coupling with Zeus was all in vain.
Summon them
so you may hear my final words,
about the prophesies I know.

Hyllos

I must now tell you this:
your mother is not here.
She's gone to Tiryns by the sea   1580

and made her home there.
And she's taken some of your children
with her, to raise them herself.
Others now live in Thebes.
But those of us here, Father,
we will hear what we must do
and serve you.

Herakles

Hear then what you must do—
now is the moment you'll show
if you're a man who can be called my son.   1590
Long ago my father Zeus
made known to me I would not die
at the hands of any living person
but a dweller in Hades.   *
And so this savage Centaur,
dead as he is, has ended my life
just as that older prophecy foretold.
And now—to go along with that one—
hear the prophecy recently revealed to me.
I wrote it down when I visited Dodona   1600*
and the grove of the Selloi,
priests who sleep on the ground
there in the mountains. I heard it
from my father's oak of many tongues.
It said that now, in this living moment,
I would be released from all my labors.
I thought that meant I would prosper.
But no, it meant I would die, nothing else.
For aren't the dead beyond labor?

So, since what was predicted is—clear as day—   1610
happening now, you, child, must help me

in this struggle.
Don't let any hesitation of yours
embitter my tongue.
Yield to me. Work with me.
Discover the best law of all:
obey your father.

Hyllos

Father, I fear where our talk is leading us,
but I will obey you.

Herakles

First, give me your right hand.   1620

Hyllos

Why demand this pledge from me?

Herakles

Do it. Don't disobey me.

Hyllos

Here is my hand . . .
I won't argue.

Herakles

Swear on the head of my father Zeus.

Hyllos

Swear what? That I'll do what? Tell me.

Herakles

That you will perform the task I'll describe.

Hyllos

As Zeus is my witness, I swear it.

Herakles

And pray you will suffer if you sidestep your oath.

Hyllos

That won't happen: I'll do as you demand.   1630
Still, I pray I'll suffer if I sidestep my oath.

Herakles

Well then.
You know the high peak of Zeus' Mount Oita?

Hyllos

Yes. I've often stood there to offer sacrifice.

Herakles

You must carry me there.
With your own hands, then, and with chosen friends

build a great pyre
from the wood of the deep-rooted oak you've cut down
along with branches from male wild olive trees.
Place my body on it. Then   1640
take torches of pine wood and set all on fire.
Let me see no tears, hear no wailing.
If you are my son, do it tearless and mute.
If you don't, I will be, from the world below,
an everlasting curse weighing you down.

Hyllos

[**cry of despair**]
Father! What have you said?
What are you doing to me?

Herakles

What must be done.
Otherwise be son to some other man.
Be called my son no longer.   1650

Hyllos

[**cry of despair**]
Oh, what you ask of me, Father!
To be your killer? *Your* blood on *my* hands?

Herakles

No! To be healer of my troubles.
Sole physician to my sickness.

Hyllos

How would I heal your body if I set it on fire?

Herakles

If you're afraid to do that, at least do the rest.

Hyllos

This I won't refuse: I'll carry you there.

Herakles

And build the pyre as I described?

Hyllos

Yes. I'll do all the rest: everything—
short of lighting it with my own hand.   1660
Whatever I do you'll find no fault in it.

Herakles

That will be enough—even that.   *
But grant me one small favor more
beyond the big ones you've granted already.

Hyllos

No matter how big, it will be done.

Herakles

Well then . . .
you know the young girl, Eurytos' daughter.

Hyllos

Iole? You mean Iole?

Herakles

Yes. This, son, is my command.
If you want to show your reverence, 1670
remember the oath you swore to your father.
When I am dead, make that girl your wife.
[**Hyllos turns away.**]
Don't disobey me, your father.
Don't let another man have her
—this woman who lay by *my* side.
Take charge of her bed yourself.
[**Hyllos continues to walk away from Herakles.**]
Obey me. For even if you trust me in great things,
to disobey in something small like this
will wipe out all the favors you've done.

Hyllos [**groaning but turning back to face Herakles**]

It's not good to be angry with a sick man, 1680
but who could bear the sight
of one who thinks such thoughts?

Herakles

You've no intention of doing what I ask?

Hyllos

Who could?
Marry the woman who of all people
shares responsibility with my mother herself
for her death?
And for the way *you yourself* are now?
Who could do that, if not crazed
by vengeful spirits? Better for me   1690
to die with you, Father,
than share a life, *a house*, with her,
the one I hate most in the world.

Herakles [to himself]

Although I am dying, it seems this man
refuses to give me my due.
[turning to Hyllos and shouting]
Know then
the curse of the gods awaits you
for disobeying my command!

Hyllos

[cry of despair]
Soon, it seems, you'll let all see how sick you are.

Herakles

Yes, for you're waking the pain that sleeps in me.   1700

Hyllos

I've nowhere to turn! Nowhere to go!

[Iole appears from inside the house and stands silently at the door.]

Herakles

No—for you think it right to disobey your creator.

Hyllos [approaching Herakles]

But, Father, must I learn to practice impiety?

Herakles

Impiety? No.
Not if what you do will gladden my heart.

Hyllos

Then *in all justice* you order me to do this?

Herakles

I do. I call on the gods to bear me witness.

Hyllos

Then I'll do it. I won't refuse.   *
But I'll show the gods the deed is yours.
Obedience to *you*, Father,   1710
could never put me in the wrong.

Herakles

At last a just conclusion.
Now add to it the gift of swiftness
and place me on the pyre
before the pain pierces me again
and rips me to bits.
[**urgently**]
Come, hurry, lift me up.
This in truth is my rest—
my rest from hard labor.
Here the man I am   1720
meets his last end.

Hyllos

Nothing prevents my doing what you ask, Father,
since you command and compel it.

Herakles [chanting]

Now, come now
before you rouse
this sickness again.
Oh stubborn spirit!
Set in this mouth
a steel bit—
turn it to stone   1730
to silence any cry.
Bring this unwanted
labor to an end
as if it were
in truth a pleasure.

Hyllos [chanting]

You who attend him
raise him up.
Show how deeply
you feel with me
for all of this.   1740
For you see how little
the gods feel
for what's happened here.
Our creators they are,
and we call them our fathers.
But they look on
indifferent
to suffering like this.
No one can see
what is to come.   1750
But what's here before us
stirs *us* to pity
and on *them* pours shame,
but for *this man*, of all men,
who endures his own ruin,
it's the greatest agony.

[**Attendants pick up Herakles' stretcher. Hyllos, the Doctor, and the attendants move off towards Mount Oita, the exit not yet used in the play. Iole watches from the doorway of the house. The Chorus Leader addresses her.**]

Chorus Leader [to Iole]   *

Girl, do not be left here,
here at the house.
Great and strange

are the deaths you've witnessed. 1760
So many sufferings
never heard of before.
And in all this there's nothing
that is not Zeus.

[Iole moves slowly, tentatively, to follow Hyllos.]

NOTES

l. 4: *"till he's dead"*: The idea that a person's life cannot be judged happy or unhappy until it is over is attributed in the first book of Herodotos' *Histories* to Solon, the Athenian statesman who lived in the sixth and early fifth centuries BCE. It was probably folk wisdom dating to a much earlier time.

ll. 11–12: Pleuron, Deianeira's home, is a town in southwest Aitolia, near the river Acheloos. Aitolia is an area of Greece west of Attica, north of the Peloponnese, and south of Thessaly.

l. 14: Rivers in Greek mythology are often personified as gods and often, like water, have the power to change shape.

l. 26: Alkmene is the mortal mother of Herakles.

l. 54: Iphitos is the son of Eurytos, the ruler of the town of Oichalia on the island of Euboia, just east of Trachis. Iphitos' sister, Iole, appears later in the play. Herakles and his family are exiled to Trachis, a town in Aitolia about two hundred miles north of their home. Exile was a common punishment for murder; in this version of the Herakles myth, it is the murder of Iphitos that has caused his family's exile to Trachis.

After l. 63ff.: The Greek word we have translated as "message" refers to a wax tablet: wax surfaces on two boards of wood that fold together. Writing is incised into the wax. In the stage directions we have called it a scroll, since the word *tablet* has other implications for a twenty-first-century audience. The message contains a prophecy, information about which is slowly revealed at lines 110ff., 216ff., 1151ff., and 1605ff. Here, at line 61ff., we learn that Deianeira has received a message from Herakles fifteen months prior to the day the play takes place. She has read the message but only hints here that it may predict a catastrophe for Herakles. At line 110ff., Deianeira reveals that the prophecy mentions Oichalia and predicts that something to do with that place will be decisive for Herakles' future. At line 216ff., she focuses not on the place but on the time when the prophecy will be relevant and repeats that he will either die or live free of trouble at that time. At line 1151ff., the chorus tells us that the prophecy was spoken twelve years prior to the time of the event it predicts, so ten years and nine months prior to Herakles' mentioning it first to Deianeira. At line 1598ff., he tells us that this prophecy, which he received at Dodona, is more recent than an earlier one he had received, saying that he would not die at the hand of a living being (ll. 1592–93). The slow and incomplete revelations of the contents of the prophecies contribute to the way the play dramatizes how impossible it is for humans to have a complete understanding of events and make decisions based on full knowledge. Many scholars also feel that the various revelations of the first oracle discussed in this note are not consistent with one another; this confusion, if it exists, may be another way that Sophokles conveys the limitations in human understanding.

After l. 68: The Nurse is a slave who probably left Pleuron with Deianeira when she married and may have been her primary caregiver as she was growing up.

l. 89: As with the captive women and Iole later in the play, the Nurse most likely became a slave when her city was invaded and conquered. Awareness that anyone's status as a free person could change to enslaved person as the cost of defeat in war may have added to the general sense of life's insecurity that Deianeira expresses in her opening lines. For a brief account of ancient slavery, see https://slaveryinjustice.wordpress.com/slavery-in-ancient-greece/.

l. 100: The Lydian woman is Omphale. In addition to his family's exile, Herakles was sold to her as a slave in punishment for killing Eurytos' son, Iphitos. This part of the story of Herakles can be found in other literary sources that predate Sophokles' play, as can the sacking of Oichalia, which Hyllos mentions at l. 108.

After l. 131: The chorus is made up of twelve or fifteen (depending on the date of the play, which is unknown) male singers and dancers representing young, unmarried girls of Trachis. Their singing and dancing are accompanied by the *aulos*, a wind instrument whose sound most resembles that of the oboe, among contemporary Western instruments. Their songs alternate with the scenes (episodes) in which actors interact. The Chorus Leader speaks the lines that the chorus exchanges with the actors in the episodes.

l. 166: A number of Greek cities claimed Herakles as native son, most prominently Argos and Tiryns in the Peloponnese and Thebes in Boiotia.

l. 182: The Great Bear is the constellation also known as the Big Dipper.

l. 236: At Dodona, an important site of prophecy in Greece, Zeus' priestesses, who interpreted the oracles delivered through the rustling of the oak leaves, were called "Doves." Their name may be a corruption of a word for "old women," the grey color and haunting song of doves making them a good representation of the priestesses.

l. 258: A herald is an official, attached to a military leader or a ruler or a governmental body, who makes public declarations and conveys official messages, much like the press secretary of the US president if he or she had to travel around the United States with the president's messages rather than calling a press conference.

l. 268: Malis is the area around Trachis, including the Bay or Gulf of Malia and its shores and the town of Thermopylae ("Warm Gates"), where the Spartans fought to the death against the invading Persian army in 480 BCE.

After l. 281: This song occurs in the middle of a scene, at a moment of high emotion at the news of Herakles' imminent return. All the other choral songs occur at the end of scenes and mark a transition from one scene to the next. There are also formal features that distinguish it from the other songs. Singing occurs at other moments in the play to convey intense emotion: for example, when the chorus sings in response to the Nurse's announcement of Deianeira's suicide and when Herakles sings to convey his despair and pain.

l. 294: A paian is a hymn of appeal or thanksgiving to Apollo, the Healer. It was also used more generally as a song of celebration or victory but occasionally also of mourning or distress.

l. 297: Ortygia is another name for the island of Delos where Leto gave birth to Apollo and Artemis.

l. 303: The *aulos* is a reed instrument with two pipes that can be played independently and simultaneously by a single musician (see also note after l. 131). To hear what the *aulos* may have sounded like, see the recording of a production of Euripides' *Herakles* at

Barnard College, in which a musician trained on a reconstruction of an *aulos* accompanies the chorus: https://www.youtube.com/watch?v=gM4sYJ7hdqg.

l. 305: The cry *euoi* is associated with the worship of the god Dionysos, as are the ivy and the "bacchic whirl" in lines 308–9.

l. 334: Kenaia is a promontory on the island of Euboia that projects westward into the Gulf of Malia. Zeus Kenaios had a sanctuary nearby. It is the place from which Herakles would set sail to reach Trachis.

l. 702: The island of Kypris (Cyprus) is sacred to the goddess Aphrodite. Kypris (Aphrodite) is one of her cult names.

l. 720: Oiniadai is a town on the banks of the river Acheloos and is the major site of the river god's worship.

l. 722: Thebes is, in some traditions, Herakles' birthplace but is also sacred to the god Dionysos (Bakkhos) as the home of Dionysos' mother, Semele, and the first town in Greece to recognize Dionysos as a god (see Euripides' *Bakkhai*). By associating Herakles with Dionysos, Sophokles may be evoking Herakles' reputation in myth as someone subject to mania and drunkenness.

l. 749: "Like a mother": Many editors dispute the authenticity of the word *mother* here because the chorus is made up of young unwed women, young enough to be Deianeira's daughters. The most common emendation offered by editors for "mother" is "spectator," which requires the change of only one letter of the Greek word for mother. In our opinion, it is not beyond the poetic imagination of the chorus to feel for Deianeira's situation as a mother would. Though not mothers themselves, they have all experienced a mother's love, and it is not uncommon for tragic characters to evoke perspectives they have not experienced directly. At lines 767–68, Deianeira, for example, imagines her grief is like the cargo a seaman takes onto his boat, although she has never been a seaman.

l. 791: The Centaurs were creatures whose forms were half-man, half-horse. On the whole, Centaurs are depicted as lustful and wild.

l. 798: The Evenos river runs from north to south through Aitolia. Herakles and Deianeira had to cross it when they left Pleuron, Deianeira's home, to travel to Herakles' home in the Argolid.

l. 820: The killing of the Hydra, a many-headed, snake-like water monster, was one of Herakles' labors, which mainly involve ridding the world of monsters that were seen as a threat to the civilized world. Herakles extracted the venom from the Hydra and used it to make his arrows more deadly. The association of Nessos with the Hydra's poison, in addition to Nessos' assault of Deianeira, allows the killing of Nessos to be seen as another of Herakles' acts to protect civilization.

l. 844: We have tried to capture the intentional ambiguity of this line in the Greek: Is the Chorus Leader saying "you must know before you act" or "you can only know by acting"?

l. 886: The god Hermes was the patron of heralds. In Homer, Hermes is often sent by Zeus to carry messages to other gods or to mortals. He carried the herald's staff (two snakes intertwined), which is also carried by human heralds. His patronage of heralds is also due to his function as the keeper and transgressor of boundaries. Heralds often carry messages across boundaries—geographical or personal. Lichas, for example, is one of the three characters in the play—the others being Hyllos and Iole—who crosses the divide between Deianeira's and Herakles' worlds. Since Hermes is also a trickster god, it is possible that his connection to heralds signals the fear of heralds' possible unreliability.

l. 909: "The Gates where assemblies of Greeks grew famous" is a reference to the meetings of the Amphictyonic League, an association of tribes from many parts of Greece that administered the oracle at Delphi. "The Gates" is a translation of the name of one of the places where the league met and is used, more generally, of the meetings themselves.

l. 910: The *aulos* is here associated, perhaps ironically, not with tragic song but with the joyous sound of the lyre. It is more usually the instrument that accompanies laments. Its sound is also associated with the god Dionysos and ecstatic states: here, the chorus's joy at the imminent return of Herakles but soon, the state of intense pain Herakles is in when he arrives.

l. 992: The simile of wine poured onto the earth alludes to the pouring of libations, a common practice at many ceremonial and religious occasions. The event Deianeira is describing, however, is the opposite of a libation, as this foam seems to be rising out of the earth and the Underworld, as a reaction to the poison seeping down, unlike the foam of the wine poured from above in a libation to the Olympian gods.

l. 1007: Chiron was a Centaur who, atypically of his kind, was a wise teacher and a healer. He was a friend of Herakles and was accidentally wounded by one of Herakles' arrows when Herakles was fighting other Centaurs (see note on l. 1490). Chiron could not be healed and could not, as the son of Kronos and so a god, die. He exchanged his life for Prometheus', allowing Prometheus to live and himself to be free of his pain by dying.

l. 1133: The Furies, or Erinyes, are implacable goddesses of vengeance and, more generally, personifications of curses.

After l. 1228: The contrast here between the chorus's singing and the Nurse's speaking highlights the chorus's shock at the news of Deianeira's suicide (see note after l. 281).

l. 1293: Suicide by the sword is generally associated with men; hanging is the method most commonly used by women. (See the Introduction for the possible implications of Deianeira's use of the sword to commit suicide.)

After l. 1346: Hyllos and the Doctor are chanting these lines in a rhythm that is often used in laments.

After l. 1369: Herakles' singing conveys the intensity of his feeling and, combined with Hyllos' and the doctor's chanting, makes this moment of Herakles' entrance particularly powerful.

ll. 1393–95: Although the mythic tradition presents Herakles as a civilizing force, cleansing the world of monsters and outlaws, it also pictures him as someone whose excessive strength and appetite can be destructive to his family and friends. This kind of duality is not uncommon for figures who are the subjects of hero cults, as Herakles was. (See the Introduction for further discussion of the ambiguity of Herakles' character.)

ll. 1436–37: Zeus' wife, Hera, is hostile to Herakles from the moment of his birth, as she is to many of Zeus' children by human women. In the mythic tradition, Herakles' labors are imposed on him by Eurystheus, a king of Argos; they either serve as expiation for Herakles' murder of his own wife Megara and their three children in a fit of madness inspired by Hera or as a way for Herakles to restore his father from exile to the throne of Argos.

l. 1438: Herakles calls the shirt that is devouring his flesh a "net of Furies," perhaps viewing it as a curse by which Deianeira has captured and destroyed him. The language recalls the murder of Agamemnon by his wife in Aeschylus' *Agamemnon.*

l. 1490: "The double-natured galloping man-horses" are the Centaurs, with whom Herakles engaged in a battle, killing many of them (see note on l. 1007).

ll. 1494–95: Herakles here refers to the labor that required him to capture the three-headed dog Cerberus, who guards the entrance to the Underworld.

ll. 1594–96: Although most critics do not question Herakles' assumption that the oracle predicted his death at the hands of Nessos, it is important to realize that it may be referring to Deianeira, who has also predeceased Herakles. (See the Introduction for further discussion of the implications of Herakles' assumption about the oracle.)

l. 1600: Dodona is a site in northwest Greece of an oracle of Zeus (see note on l. 64ff.). The Selloi were a tribe living near Dodona who provided priests for Zeus' oracle in its early stages. Later the oracles were interpreted by priestesses called "Doves" (see note on l. 236).

l. 1662: In the mythic tradition, it is Philoktetes (or his father) who lights the pyre. Herakles gives him his bow in gratitude. In Sophokles' play, *Philoktetes*, which was probably written after *Women of Trachis*, Herakles appears as a *deus ex machina* to persuade Philoktetes to take the bow to Troy, where it is needed to conquer the city, and be healed there of his festering leg wound. In *Philoktetes*, it is clear that Herakles has been saved from the pyre and deified by his father Zeus. In this play, there is no mention of Herakles' apotheosis, although critics have found hints of it at several points in the play. Sophokles leaves it to each member of the audience to imagine whether or not Herakles dies on the pyre and what the consequences of each possible end are for the play. (See the Introduction for further discussion about the question of the apotheosis.)

l. 1708: The Spartans claim the descendants of Hyllos and Iole, the Heraclidae, as the founders of their royal family. At the time *Women of Trachis* was written (the date is unknown), Athens may already have been anticipating their war with the Spartans (the Peloponnesian War) that ended in Athenian defeat. How this historical circumstance may have affected the audience's view of this moment in the play is interesting to consider.

After l. 1756: Both the text of these final lines and their attribution to a speaker are uncertain because of variations in the surviving manuscripts of the play and thus are matters of disagreement among scholars:

1. *Who speaks these final lines?* Many editors attribute these lines to Hyllos, arguing that although the final lines of the surviving tragedies are spoken by the chorus, in this play, the chorus has been silent for three hundred lines, and it would be jarring to have them speak again at the end of the play (although they are on stage and, by convention, might be expected to speak).

   We feel that these words should be spoken by the chorus of young women, bringing a female voice back into the play at its end and maintaining what seems to be a consistent convention across extant tragedies of allowing the chorus to signal the end of the play.

2. *Who is the "girl" to whom they are addressed?* If Hyllos is the speaker, the "girl" is probably the chorus addressed in the singular—strange but possible. If the chorus speaks these lines, the "girl" may be themselves or Iole. We have chosen to have the chorus address Iole.

   Although there is no indication that Iole has entered the stage from the house and although characters' entrances and exits are almost always marked by a comment from someone on stage, as a silent character throughout the play, Iole's role is already unusual. In Aeschylus' *Agamemnon*, of which there are echoes in *Women of Trachis*, Cassandra enters the stage and remains silently there without being acknowledged for 150 lines. It seems perfectly possible that a silent character's entrance may go unannounced. Moreover, Iole is the only character to whom the singular address "girl" is fitting. In addition, she is the only character of whom it can rightly be said that she has witnessed "great and strange deaths." This phrase is usually understood to refer to Deianeira's death, which in fact no one has witnessed, although Iole, unlike the chorus, was at least in the house when she died there. But Iole has also witnessed the destruction of her family and her city.

3. *Is the girl being told not to be "left here, / here at the house" or not to be left away from the house (the readings of the manuscripts differ)?* If the girl is being told not to be left away from the house, the end of the play reinforces the separation of the male and female worlds we have seen throughout: the men depart for Mount Oita, and Iole (and the chorus) return to the house, the realm of the female. If she is being told not to be left in the house, and we see her start to depart with Hyllos and Herakles up to Mount Oita, the final moment of the play perhaps offers a different possibility for the way Iole and Hyllos will shape their future. (See the Introduction for a further discussion of this possibility.)

CAST LIST FOR AUDIO RECORDING

To hear the audio recording of a performance of Sophokles' *Women of Trachis,* translated by Rachel Kitzinger and Eamon Grennan, visit the open access version of this book at https://doi. org/10.3998/mpub.12159971. All members of the cast are students at Vassar College.

Director: Abigail Lass
Sound engineer: Pedro Lima
Chorus directors: Tessa Hyatt
                   Phineas Hillard

In order of appearance:

Deianeira: Eden Bartholomew
Nurse: Jen Jacobs
Hyllos: Jack Francis
Chorus Leader: Lena Pepe
Chorus: Keira DiGaetano
         Elizabeth Perkins
         Emily Wadholm
         Chelsea Zak

Messenger: Doruk Evcim
Lichas: Noah Hornick
Doctor: Phineas Hillard
Herakles: Ethan Balfour Clark

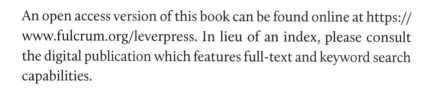

An open access version of this book can be found online at https://www.fulcrum.org/leverpress. In lieu of an index, please consult the digital publication which features full-text and keyword search capabilities.

9 781643 150307